MAYAN JADE

BY

S. M. CWALINSKI

one

Xuxmal looked nervously over his shoulder as he scrambled and shoved his way through the dark and forbidding jungle, torn between wanting to be quick and needing to be quiet. He wanted to be in his spot before the sun rose, before the Temple Guards, who seemed to have eyes and ears everywhere, could arrive and take up their positions, jealously guarding even the view of the sacred pyramids from peasants such as himself. For today was a special day, a day of sacrifice to the gods that Xuxmal thought must be especially cruel to demand the death of such a young and innocent girl to persuade them to bring the corn. And even with the blood of the virgin to fertilize the temple it was still a struggle to bring the crop out of the rocky soil of the ever-encroaching jungle, harder and harder each year to feed the people of his village and meet the demands of the priests and nobles. And yet somehow he was drawn to watch, to risk his life just to get a glimpse of her final and fatal ascension up the brilliantly colored and awesomely massive pyramid, to the lethal ministrations of the High Priest. He could feel the sting of his sweat rolling down into the many scratches on his body from the sharp edged plants of the unforgiving jungle as he settled into the small crevice in some rocks that he had discovered one day while hunting monkeys. The first rays of the rising sun glared into his eyes as he peered through the gaps in the dense jungle canopy at the steep steps of the most holy pyramid.

Tuamanuca shifted his weight from one foot to the other as he stood in the shade of the tall trees on the edge of the sandy path that led to Xuxmal's village. He knew the lure of the awesome spectacle about to unfold in the Temple square would be too great for some foolish peasants to resist. After all, it had it all, color, pageantry, blood and even death, with a strong dose of mysticism and fear thrown in. He felt he could feel their fear, even smell it, and if he could catch one of the ignorant bastards and bring him in to be executed it would greatly enhance his position in the Guards. So he tried to sink deeper into the shadows of the dank and humid jungle as he diligently scanned the dense canopy of trees in the direction that would give the best view of the pyramids, eager to do his duty should the opportunity arise.

Suddenly, farther in the dark and virgin jungle, where even the braver villagers like Xuxmal never ventured, El Tigre, who was the true lord of this land before man's so called civilization had risen, and who would be again after these supposedly eternal constructions had fallen into ruin, voiced his anger at these human disturbances to his kingdom with a scream so horrible that both men jerked in fear and began sweating a sweat of terror far deeper than anything the priests could inspire.

*　　　　*　　　　*

Mitch strolled casually along the crowded sidewalk, his six foot height defeating his desire not to stand out among the locals, occasionally stopping to check out the wares of the shops lining the busy street in the Mercado district. He went in and out of the little shoe repair shop, the open-front hammock and shirt store, bought a soda at the ma and pop café on the corner, all the while holding onto the embroidered cloth bag from Guatemala that was slung over his shoulder. He smiled and laughed as he spoke to the people in the shops but he didn't feel as casual as he appeared. He felt as if someone was watching him, studying him as he went, and he actually had good reason to feel that way, because the Guatemalan bag contained several illegally obtained, illegal to even *possess*, artifacts from the Mayan ruins that Mitch had just visited. Mitch hadn't stolen them or even found them himself, he was just a delivery boy for the local traders who bought and sold the relics, at a nice profit, to whoever would pay the price asked. Mitch had been in-country long enough to speak Spanish without an American accent, to know his way around and to have spent all the money he had brought with him. The money wasn't his only motivation though, because Mitch considered himself an adventurer, a free spirit who would do whatever he thought would get him further down the "Gringo Trail" without violating his rather broad moral philosophy or landing him in jail. He definitely was nervous about this little scam though, and his nervousness took a major leap when he saw the two city cops on the corner he was approaching. He hesitated just a bit, trying to decide whether to turn around or go ahead and balls it out when suddenly he felt a hand on his shoulder, not hard, not grabbing him, but enough to make him stop. He turned to see a stocky, well dressed Mexican smiling calmly as he smoothly brought a black wallet out of his expensive looking overcoat and opened it to briefly flash a gold badge.

"You're not thinking of running, are you amigo?" the detective said as he moved in front of Mitch to block his path.   "No way, sir," Mitch replied, especially since he could see two more uniformed cops hustling up the street behind them, "But I would like to know who I am talking to and why."

"I'm Inspector Dada, and this is why,"

the detective replied with a cold and unsettling smile as he lifted the cloth bag off of Mitch's shoulder, feeling its weight, "And I think we need to continue this conversation downtown, okay?"

Inspector Dada let Mitch spend the rest of that day and most of the next in the holding cell of the downtown headquarters, probably just to let him know he could, to show Mitch he was a stranger in the Inspector's territory and wouldn't have all the "rights" he might have tried to assert in his own country. Mitch had been in-country long enough not to need any reminders of the trouble he was in, and he also knew that the state prison where he could wind up was nothing like the modern. air-conditioned jail in this downtown building. But he wasn't a complete fool, and knew he wasn't as nailed as this arrogant little man thought he was, so it was with a bit of a confident swagger that he followed the guards down the polished corridors to Dada's office and sat in the chair across from the desk to wait for the detective, curious to see what his reaction would be. Mitch didn't have long to wait because it was obvious as the Inspector came striding rapidly into the room and slammed the Guatemala bag on the desk that he was furious, barely able to contain his anger. He fixed his dark eyes on Mitch like an angry lion as he stood over him and said,

"You think you are pretty damn clever, don't you, gringo?"

Mitch calmly looked up at him as Dada abruptly dumped the artifacts out of the bag onto his desk, the hard clay statuettes clattering loudly in the quiet room. "These are legal, just cheap souvenirs that anyone could buy!" Mitch didn't say a word but he was thinking, *"No shit, Sherlock."* He had been wondering how long it would take for this supercilious asshole to figure that out.

"So, where did you make the switch, wiseguy? Come on, we were following you for quite a while and my men are searching every shop you went into right now, and we will find your partners soon enough. So, make it easy on yourself and tell us which one it was." Dada said this very menacingly and convincingly but both men knew that the real artifacts were long gone and that Dada's agents would find nothing.   "I'm sure I don't know what you're talking about," Mitch said as he coolly met Dada's angry glare, "I'm just into Mayan lore, that's all." The Inspector grunted and clenched and unclenched his fists as he walked around the desk and sat heavily in his chair, unbuttoning his fine sport coat as he leaned back. He studied Mitch carefully, then took a deep breath and let it out slowly as he closed his eyes to think. When he opened them he was completely composed, calm and deliberate as he leaned forward to speak.

"Ok, Mitch, it is Mitch, right? Mitch Kowalski from Florida, let us talk together as men, men of the world, okay? You pulled off a pretty clever little stunt out there yesterday, you know that and I know that, and you know I probably can't nail you on it, right? Right. But I can still make life miserable for you, you know. If I bring charges I can hold you for weeks, maybe months, and you'd have to get a lawyer and all that, this is my country after all, right, amigo?" Mitch leaned forward to speak, hoping his increasing nervousness didn't show, not feeling half the defiant bravado he had felt earlier. He knew the traders he was working for wouldn't bail him out because he was just a mule and didn't know enough to really hurt them even if he spilled his guts completely, and he knew that what Dada had said was true, that Dada could mess with him all he wanted and there wasn't much he could do about it. He didn't know where this was going and that scared him but he tried to sound confident as he said,

"That's true, it's your country, but I am an American after all, and I could call the Embassy to see what they have to say about this fiasco." Mitch instantly realized this wasn't the way to go as he saw the flash of anger in the Inspector's eyes, "But," he said quickly, "I am a law abiding citizen and I always like to cooperate with law enforcement wherever I go." Mitch was glad to see Dada relax a little and even smile at that one. "So, where do we go from here?" he asked innocently.

Inspector Dada smiled more broadly now and said, "You can go back to your *pension* now and relax. Just don't try to leave town, okay?"

*   *   *

"Damn, this Dada character sure believes in letting people cool their heels while he's got them on a string," thought Mitch as he shook the raindrops off his Levi jacket before hanging it on a peg on the wall. The late afternoon rain had brought him back to his *pension*, the Hotel Astoria, from a long, rambling walking tour of the city. Tovelado was one of Mitch's favorite types of town in Central America, an old Spanish colonial town now populated by a lively mix of Mayan Indians, descendants of the great civilizations of the pyramid builders, aware and proud of their heritage, and modern Mexicans, both rich and poor, all going about their business with an energy and pace that didn't jive with the 'siesta' image of Latin culture held by many North Americans. Since Tovelado was the capitol of the department, or state, it had it's share of large, modern buildings, several stories of concrete, steel, and glass, usually housing banks or office complexes, sometimes with department stores on the ground floor. Taxis pulled up in the right lane of the two and four lane boulevards to let fashionably dressed women out to shop in the up-to-date boutiques while conservatively suited businessmen clutched their leather and black briefcases, hurrying to their next appointment. Yet within blocks of this modern urban center began a cosmopolitan sprawl of old world flavor and new world energy. From the central Mercado, where everything you could think of was sold in either open air booths or tiny stalls in the warren-like main building, to the ubiquitous street vendors selling ice cream or oranges or candy on every corner, there was an incredible richness and color to the fabric of life here. And the Astoria fit right in, being known up and down the "Gringo Trail" as a backpacker's hotel, a place that catered to gringo travelers who were just passing through, usually going second class to stretch their money as many miles and as many countries as it would go. It was run by a husband and wife team and although it was a decades old wood frame building, they were very proud of it and kept it up well. Many applications of the pastel blue shade of paint had coated the outside, and the wood floor inside shone from the repeated sweeping and polishing done by the couple's two daughters. The office in the front hall doubled as the registration desk and base for a small money changing operation run by the husband. He was a friendly guy who could give you directions to just about any place in the city as well as a good exchange rate. The rest of the first floor was dominated by the kitchen, run by *La Cochina*, the cook, with the autocratic disdain of a person who knows how important they are, and several tables and chairs that made up a little cantina. To order something you had to go stand by the kitchen door, a double door with the lower half closed, until *la cochina* decided to notice you. Then you asked politely for *beefstica con arroz con plaintains* (beefsteak and delicious fried bananas), which she would cook sometime soon when she felt like it. There was no pushing the cook at all, but Mitch didn't mind because the fast food mentality of the 'States was one of the things he wanted to get away from. The fact that the bathroom was down the hall from the bedrooms upstairs or that the shower was lit by a naked light bulb with questionable wiring didn't bother Mitch much either because an afternoon at the Astoria was worth more than a ton of travel brochures as far as finding out about places you wanted to go. The place was clean, cheap, and a great source of information about the hazards and pleasures of the road north and south, because you could talk to people who had actually been to the place in question, and been there recently. The good comradeship of the "Trail", the easy temporary partnerships, the sitting around all afternoon drinking coffee and swapping road stories, were some of the good things that had brought Mitch back to the gringo trail. As Mitch was sitting down with his cup of coffee he noticed a couple in the hall, folding their umbrellas and shaking the rain off their coats. The man was tall, early forties, with black curly hair just tinged with gray, and he stood very straight as he took in the room, nodding at Mitch as he hung up his coat. The woman...his wife or daughter perhaps...was much younger, somewhere around twenty, and an outstanding example of local beauty. She had long, straight, pitch black hair, lush and heavy, shiny like a Polynesian girl's. Her eyes were as dark as her hair and offset by the unblemished smoothness of her skin over her high cheekbones. Those cheekbones and the roundness of her chin showed some Indian influence in her background somewhere. Mitch, proud of the smidgeon of Cherokee blood on his mother's side of the family, couldn't understand why many Latin Americans sought to downplay the Indian side of their heritage. "The mix sure produced some women as fine as you could ask for," Mitch thought as he watched them come toward his table.

"Excuse me," the man said in Spanish," could you tell me, are there many other people staying here?"

"Yes, but they are off in various directions today," Mitch replied in his rough Spanish.

"You are American, right?" the girl cut in, "We will speak in English, all right?"

"Yes , yes, of course," the man said, "I'm Doctor Comacho, and this is my daughter, Elena." Mitch stood up and gave each his hand, nodding politely, "Mitch Kowalski, from Florida, please sit down."

"Didn't I read about you in the paper?" Mitch asked as they sat, "Aren't you leading an expedition into the jungle, or something like that?"

"We are supposed to be," Dr. Comacho replied, "Did you also read about the group of graduate students that was coming with us?"

"Well, I read the paper for practice in Spanish but I really don't get it all," Mitch said. "Why?"

"Because it is not true," the girl exclaimed, her dark eyes glowing. Mitch watched the flush of blood rise up her graceful neck and over those beautiful cheeks. "The government was going to pay their travel expenses and everything and now they have withdrawn their support."

"Calm down, daughter," the professor said, raising one finger in a gesture Mitch had seen from some of his teachers in school, "Why don't you go see if the cook will make us some café, okay?"

It was with considerable difficulty that Mitch shifted his attention away from the figure of Elena as she strode energetically toward the kitchen, her long black hair bouncing and her firm young body taut under her no-nonsense business skirt. But the professor himself had a kind of intensity

that held one's attention. He gave Mitch the impression of a man on a crusade, a true believer, not a fanatic like the Bible-beaters who came to Mitch's door back home, more, it seemed to Mitch, to reinforce their own faith than to change his, or a phony, like the television ministers making themselves rich while spreading the Word, but a man totally wrapped up in his mission, his beliefs.

"And a man willing to work at it," thought Mitch, noticing that in spite of the professor's expensive clothes and aristocratic bearing, he had the tanned and lined face, the crow's feet around the eyes, and calluses on the strong hands of a man who spent at least some of his time outdoors , working. Mitch's impression of a man on a mission was confirmed as soon as Dr. Comacho started talking, leaning towards Mitch across the table, his dark eyes looking steadily into Mitch's.

"Elena is overexcited, Senor. The government did not withdraw its support, just cut it back enough so that all of our assistants must be volunteers, as there is no money to pay their way here." The Professor lowered his head, "Those graduate students will work to learn, but I was hoping for more than just cheap help. I wanted those young people to have the experience of meeting their past head-on. Many people seem to feel our history starts with the Spanish Conquistadores; that the Indian ruins and relics are great for tourists but don't really relate to us today. Some even seem to be embarrassed by the non-Spanish side of our heritage."

"But Father is going to change all that, "Elena broke in, returning with two cups and a pot of coffee, "We are going to put together an exhibit from this dig, and tour the country, giving lectures, maybe write a book . . ."

"Wait a minute," the professor laughed,

"First we have to get some results out of the expedition, and to do that we need help. So, tell me, Mitch, is this *pension* a good spot to recruit?"   "Well, there's the California agricultural students, but they have their own project." Mitch sat back and tried to guess how the other tenants at the Astoria would feel about this trip, "There is a couple from England, but I think that they are on some sort of schedule; wait a minute, maybe Teodore. Teo is a German guy who is studying Mayan culture in college; he's over here just to see ruins, he might want to go. I can't promise anything but I'll talk to him; and maybe Louis, the Canadian, he is on a flexible schedule."

"What about yourself, Senor?" asked Elena, "What are your plans?"

"Wait a minute, Elena, don't be impolite . . . we don't want to press," said Dr. Comacho sternly .

"It's all right, Doc," replied Mitch, looking into Elena's direct and steady gaze, "I'll give the matter some serious consideration."

"Fine," said the Professor, "We can be reached at the Hotel Royale. We must know within two days, Senor, and I hope we will be hearing from you. Adios"

"Sure, sure, *buenos dias*, and good luck," said Mitch as they got up and turned to go. "What a classy pair," he thought. And that could apply either to the couple or her legs. "Either way I wouldn't mind some further association."

*   *   *

Mitch and Louis stepped into the cool, crisp air of early evening, paused to adjust their packs, then headed down to the bus stop. They had paid their bills at the Astoria and said amicable good-byes to the proprietor and the all-important cook. They told each other they would stay at the Astoria if they were ever through here again, but they both knew it wasn't very likely, since all the travelers on the Gringo Trail hated to backtrack.   Mitch looked at Louis walking beside him; carrying all that gear he looked even smaller than he actually was.

"Small but wiry," thought Mitch, "He must be pretty tough to make it this far." Louis had been on the road for six months already, coming across the United States from Canada, where he had picked apples for six months to get the money to travel. Six months of ten to twelve hour days six days a week, stuck on an orchard out in the boonies. But they paid well and since there weren't many places to spend your money it was easy to save. Louis's ultimate goal was to reach Tierra del Fuego on the southern tip of South America, but since he had the time and the means to do it, the Professor's expedition was just what he liked. To meet the people who lived in these out of the way places, to really get to know the country and its culture was a desire that Mitch and Louis had in common with most of the young travelers on the "trail". Teodore, the German guy, was a slightly different case. He was a serious student of archeology and anthropology who was doing a thesis on the Mayans.   His trip to Central America was the big event of his scholarship so far. To actually be there, at the ruins themselves, to see and feel those vast magnificent constructions of another age put new life into the dry and dusty studies of the University. Mitch felt that Teodore would jump at the chance to work with the professor but he didn't know for sure. He had told Teo about it and had gotten him in touch with Dr Comacho. Mitch didn't want the responsibility of talking anyone into taking the trip, since he wasn't sure if he would be able to go either, what with the situation of the fake artifacts and Inspector Dada. But Mitch was pleasantly surprised and somewhat puzzled when Dada said it was OK, just keep him informed and don't leave the country. Mitch didn't know why Inspector Dada had changed his attitude but he wasn't going to argue about it. He had decided he wanted to go, telling himself that it would be a good idea to get out in the bushes and let things cool off for a while.

"Well, amigo, there's the bus station," said Louis," and look, there is Teodore!" Mitch looked through the plate glass windows of the modern downtown terminal. He was glad to see Teo there; with him were a couple of other gringo backpackers and about a half a dozen Latins, presumably the graduate students. They all seemed a little uncomfortable and when Mitch and Louis walked in they could hear why. Elena was engaged in a shouting match

with the man behind the counter. Mitch picked up enough of it so that he knew it had something to do with the bus they were taking. Dr Comacho was behind the counter speaking on the telephone, one hand over his ear to block out the shrill voices of Elena and the ticket agent. Dr Comacho put down the phone and went to the counter.

"Elena, go and sit down," he commanded. She stopped shouting and turned away, but not before giving the ticket agent a look that would have fried your plaintains. She marched over and joined their little group, her small, firm breasts bouncing with her quick stride as the Professor spoke calmly and quietly with the agent. Mitch thought she was even more beautiful when she was angry but he didn't say anything. He laughed to himself as he thought,

"That would be like doing my Humphrey Bogart imitation, 'You're beautiful when you're mad, kid'." So he just stood there feeling as uncomfortable as everyone else. Dr Comacho shook the ticket agent's hand and apologized as he picked up a stack of tickets the man had written out. He came over and stood in front of Elena.

"Daughter," he said, "I'm in charge here and I'll have no more outbursts, understand?"

"Yes, Father," replied Elena in a small voice, "I'm sorry but . . ." The Professor cut her off with a raised palm and a stern look.

"What seems to be the trouble, Doc?" asked Mitch.   "Oh, we were not able to get the charter bus we anticipated, but we have gotten tickets for everyone on the regularly scheduled run," said Dr Comacho, "It is enough." Elena grabbed Mitch's arm as they all stood up to load onto the bus.

"Father is to easy," she whispered angrily, "Originally we were supposed to fly to the ruins, then we were promised a charter bus, and we wind up with this! Someone in the

Ministry must be putting money in his pocket," she fumed, "And Father just accepts it."

"Well, this isn't so bad," Mitch said soothingly, "We'll get there."

"Yes, but you haven't had the ride out there yet," said Elena, "You'll see."

Chapter Two: The Ride

The first five hours weren't so bad. In less than an hour they were beyond the outskirts of the city and into the low, rolling hills of the countryside. They had departed in the late evening and as it got later they had the road practically to themselves, just a few trucks trying to make time blasting through the night the only other traffic. About the only complaint that Mitch had was that their driver also seemed to want to make time, barreling down the narrow two-lane road at what seemed to be unnecessary speed. Mitch was glad that at least he seemed to know the road, slowing down for tight turns or a particularly rough railroad crossing. The bus drivers in Central America were all pretty competent, at least the ones that Mitch had ridden with, but it didn't do much for your confidence when they crossed themselves getting on or kissed the picture of Jesus or the rosaries they almost all carried on their buses. On some of the bus routes in the mountains there was no regular run, just the first bus at each stop would pick up the people waiting there. When one bus stopped to pick up passengers another would fly by trying to beat him to the next stop; so you often had two or three buses racing down the same narrow, twisting mountain roads all out, cutting blind corners and taking risks to get to the people first. Naturally you could often read in the paper of whole busloads of people dying when a bus went over the edge. In many parts of Central America whenever there was a fatal crash on a highway a cross was erected on the spot to commemorate the victims. Some of the mountain highways were lined with crosses, old and new, standing starkly white against the green grass on the shoulders that the locals used for free grazing for their animals.   "Oh, well," thought Mitch, "Maybe I had better start saying a little prayer for myself when I get on." Often the bus was the best and cheapest way of getting around in this part of the world. Some of the buses were very old, though. That was Mitch's other complaint; many of the buses still running on Central American highways had seen many years service on North American roads first. As a matter of fact the bus they were riding in was an old Bluebird, built and used in the United States as a school bus probably twenty-five or thirty years ago. Being built to carry students a short distance only, it was not real big on comfort. Actually, if Mitch sat straight up in the seat, with his hips backed up all the way, his knees still hit the back of the seat in front of him. While most of the locals did not approach Mitch's six foot height, it wasn't much of a problem for them, but Mitch, and Teodore, who was tall also, had to constantly shift their weight from one buttock to the other. This was getting old after just the five hours of paved road when sometime early in the morning the bus pulled off onto a dirt road and into a gas station. Mitch looked out the window in the gray light to watch the action in the gas station. Most of the so-called highways in this area were really just two-lane blacktops stretching interminably through rolling hills or pasture land, but often through dense, prolific jungle, broken only by the small plots scratched out of the thick brush by local farmers practicing slash and burn agriculture. That didn't mean there weren't towns, though. Every once in a while the bus would slow as it came into the outskirts of these little municipalities, marked by a shift from the stick and thatch huts of the Indian farmers to the concrete and plaster shops and houses of the townspeople, usually with a church of the colonial type near the center of town. There were also in most cases side streets, unpaved rock roads leading somewhere off into the fields or jungle, and there were almost always little groups of people, two or three maybe, standing at the intersection of the highway and the rock road waiting for the bus. Mitch always wondered where these people had come from and where they were going, standing there in front of a street of thatched shacks wearing their best designer jeans and stylish shirts, carrying a portable radio or stereo cassette player blaring out modern Spanish rock music, or maybe a couple of older men, wearing work clothes with pieces of rope for belts, an old straw hat or maybe a baseball cap, carrying machetes or even an old shotgun or twenty-two rifle. People like this seemed to get off and on at every stop. Where were they going, and who had ironed the crisp white shirts and blue pants or skirts of the kids going to the Catholic schools?

"These people have one foot in the twentieth century and one foot in the nineteenth," mused Mitch as he caught Teo's eye and shook his head in sympathy as he watched the tall German stretch and rub his haunches, trying to get some circulation going. He looked back out the window at the gas pumps, the bright lights of the station sign giving a strange clarity to the scene in the early morning light. Gas stations were like outposts along these roads away from the capitol, isolated and sparsely supplied, always complete with a pile of old tires, empty fifty-five gallon fuel drums and several locals hanging out, fussing with their machetes and telling stories as they sat on the old tires. Mitch always liked to watch what went on because it wasn't too unusual for a traveler to reach his destination only to find that his luggage had gotten off before he did. Things looked pretty cool to Mitch this time and he turned from watching the driver watching the gas station attendant to see Elena smoothing her slacks as she stood up by her seat.

"Now it starts," Elena said as she came back and stood by Mitch's seat, "See how the highway goes ninety degrees in that direction, Senor?"

"Si, Senorita Comacho," replied Mitch, peering into the darkness down the highway and shifting his weight again, "How much longer will we be riding?"

"Oh, ten or eleven hours, that's all," said Elena with a wry smile, "Only we are going that way." She pointed off to the right down the dirt road that Mitch thought just led to the gas pumps, "And call me Elena, por favor." She smiled sweetly at Mitch as she turned to go back to her seat. Mitch's momentary elation at the thought of Elena's smile faded quickly when he looked down the road she had pointed out.

Unpaved, narrow, it looked like the roads his father used to take him and his brothers and friends out hunting on when they were young back in Florida, out away from the rampant development of the Gold Coast. Not really dirt, but a coral rock base with rocks and loose dirt on top, with big potholes and washouts with sharp coral protruding from them. It was the kind of road that punished tires, shocks and passengers if you tried to take them at more than a crawl.

"Ten hours," thought Mitch. He could hardly believe it, "And this bus doesn't even seem to have shocks at all!" The bus driver slowed some but not much, and the bouncing they were taking was pretty rough. The bus had no air-conditioning and as it was quite cool outside almost all the windows were up. It was already stuffy and close in the crowded bus and things got worse as the bumping started to make some people carsick.

"As much as the people liked spicy foods," thought Mitch, "You might just figure that they would be used to it." But this was not the case. Bicarbonate of Soda is as much a national drink in many countries as the cervezas and tequilas are. The young couple across the aisle from Mitch was really suffering. Now that it was getting towards full morning he could see through the foggy gray light that the belching that Mitch had assumed was from the man was from the petite young woman. She was belching as loudly as a sea-sick sailor and drinking Bi-carb out of a thermos bottle. Mitch tried to blot their proximity out of his mind as he put his head down on the seat in front of him and tried to doze. He didn't really sleep but he did seem to get off to a kind of never-never land where time passed a little more quickly. When Mitch came out of it the day was full light and they had passed out of the rolling hills into a mountainous jungle. They stopped to wait for a ferry in a little village that sprawled on both sides of a wide, flowing river. A woman was washing clothes by hand in the river while a couple of naked children played in the shallows nearby, while all around the bus were woman and children, holding up their wares; chicken, oranges, shrimp, but most were holding a fried fish, whole; head, eyes, the complete thing on a platter with some fried potatoes. It must have been local fish and probably very fresh, but Mitch couldn't get himself to eat any after the night's ride. He settled for a semi-cold soda as they rode the ferry across the river. Mitch wished some of the people back home in the midst of their throw - away society could see this ferry. Easily built as far back as the thirties, if not sooner, this rusty old steel floating platform pushed confidently against the current across the river to the landing on the other side. It could only handle one bus at a time but it old diesel chugged powerfully across every trip.

"And you can't get a car to last four or five years nowadays," thought Mitch, "Planned obsolescence, supposedly good for the economy." Besides the wonder of it still functioning, Mitch was amazed that it was even here. What an effort must have gone into getting it all the way up-river; what entrepreneur or government official saw the need for it here, carrying maybe four buses a day peak, and convinced others of the need and made it happen?

"I sure admire the pioneer spirit that got this ferry placed way out here," Mitch said to Teodore standing next to him on the rail.

"Yeah, I know what you mean, but do you know who I really admire?" said Teo, ruefully rubbing his haunches, "The guy who built the airport at the ruins." The rest of the day was pure hell. As the day wore on it became hotter and hotter inside the bus. And the terrible road wound on interminably. It became one of those times when you just can't stand it anymore but there is nowhere to go and nothing you can do but endure it. So you endure it. The road was only wide enough for one bus, with no shoulders, and they were in a fairly mountainous region now. The driver kept up a pretty good pace, still pushing. Mitch was torn between wanting him to slow down for safety and comfort and wanting him to keep pushing to get the trip over with. Every little village or town they went through the ubiquitous vendors came out, not so much fish now as fruit, candy, or chicken with rice. There were even guys selling ice cream from coolers mounted on the front of their bicycles.

"There must be a generator somewhere," said Louis, "It might not be too clean, but it looks cold and I'm having some." Mitch and Louis bought some and it was delicious, very sweet with little pebbles of ice all through it. Every larger town they passed through had a junkyard on its outskirts full of wrecked cars and always at least one destroyed bus. That was great for a passenger's confidence. But they were lucky; only once, when they were careening around a blind curve, their driver almost went off the road and over the cliff because there was a broken down bus in the road. Mitch's driver just kept going, tooting his horn to the other driver to let him know that they would send help back to them when they reached the next town big enough to have a garage. Mitch looked back at the people sitting and standing in the dust by the side of the road.   "Their sixteen hour trip is going to take two days," he said to Louis, "I guess we're lucky, if you can call it that."

"Yeah," replied Louis, "But did you notice that they were all locals? I figure the touristas all fly in."

"Yeah, said Mitch, glancing up to where the Professor was sitting, "I wonder what the deal is with our guy?"

"Well, I guess we'll find out eventually," answered Louis, shaking his head.

"I hope so," Mitch said quietly, "I hope so."

They finally ground slowly down a hill and around a curve and pulled up in front of a little frame building that housed the local military. It seemed like everywhere you went there was at least some military presence. They all had to present themselves to the officer in charge and be checked out before being allowed into what amounted to a national park. The rest of the area encompassing the ruins consisted of a coral runway hacked out of the jungle, a couple of tourist hotels with their own generators and wells, two cantinas and a campground tight up against the surrounding rain forest. The ruins themselves were surrounded by thick vegetation but a system of wide, well-marked paths had been laid out for the tourists to get to the major, cleared monuments. Dr Comacho's group was to stay in the campground and to that end he had arranged for a truck loaded with supplies, tents, and other gear to meet them there. Mitch was so glad to get out of the bus that he pitched right in with the unloading. Most of the gear was old, army surplus, but still serviceable. Mitch had done quite a bit of camping but it was always backpacking style, with a tiny pup tent.

"I've always wanted to set up a base camp like this, "He said to Teo," it reminds me of being on safari in Africa or something."

"Yeah, but we're not on safari, we're going to live here." replied Teo.

"And work here, remember?" laughed Louis.

Most of the camp was finished by nightfall and everyone simply grabbed a place to sleep and fell out, exhausted. Some preferred hammocks slung in the open "chickees", which are like half open shacks made of sticks with roofs of thatched palm leaves, clustered in the campground, while others laid their sleeping bags on the old, musty cots in the tents. Bathroom facilities consisted of a double-doored chickee with a large, deep hole in the middle and makeshift planks to help you keep your balance and avoid falling in. And a trip to the john at night could be painful if you walked through a stream of army ants while coming or going. Walking at a brisk pace across their path resulted in about a half a dozen quarter inch long ants up your pant leg. They were so tough that merely slapping them against your leg wouldn't kill them. Each ant, with its massive mandibles for biting, had to be individually captured and crushed and each bite left a large red swelling. Enough of them could kill a person and they certainly traveled in sufficient numbers. Mitch resolved to stay in bed once he was comfortable and not take any late night walks.

The next day they were up early putting the finishing touches on the camp. Breakfast was fruit and bread because the gas stoves were still being set up under one of the large tents. Everyone worked eagerly to be finished with the camp so that they could go to the ruins. Dr Comacho had promised to give a guided tour, not where they were going to be working, but the main pyramids. Teo especially was looking forward to the lecture tour very much and several of the grad students had notebooks and one had a tape recorder as they set out along the path to the ruins. Monkeys scampered through the canopy of trees overhead and macaws and toucans screeched as they clumsily flew away. The toucans with their oversized beaks were especially funny to watch because when they came flying in to land in a tree they had a lot of trouble controlling the momentum of their large beaks and often crashed forward onto their faces or missed the limb entirely and just grabbed the nearest one. Once the little group of scholars had to backtrack to avoid a flow of army ants across the path. Within a few minutes they came to the large, cleared area around the largest pyramids, the solid, tangible objects of many years interest and study for many of them. The grad students pushed forward to be closer to Dr Comacho, eager to hear his every word.

Chapter Three: The Mayans

Mitch blinked as they came out of the shade of the jungle canopy and into the bright sun of the cleared and meticulously mowed central plaza. He pulled his Ray-ban aviator shades off his collar, wiped the lenses on the bottom of his shirt and put them on as the Professor went over to talk to the guard in the gatehouse. There was no charge for the professor and his group but the state did charge the tourists, most of whom came from the two bungalow style hotels between the campground and the ruins, brought around to the gatehouse at the end of the parking lot by small jeep- towed trams provided by the hotels. Mitch didn't know what they needed a parking lot for, having seen the road from the capitol and understanding that the road going the other way into Belize was a little shorter but just as rough. In fact most travelers did arrive by plane on the coral strip outside the park, usually picked up by their hotels, and spending much of their time there in the coolness and comfort of the bar except for coming out for guided tours of the pyramids. To Mitch's surprise there were a few vehicles there, though. There were a couple of dusty, battered old Volkswagen vans, the ubiquitous choice of intrepid road explorers everywhere, a jaunty and fairly new jeep with a roll bar and a convertible top, the type that newlyweds and other foolishly confident North American drivers rented in the major tourist towns, and an old but clean Chevy pick-up that probably belonged to the head groundskeeper. Also hanging out in the gatehouse area were several young boys, the ever-present vendors bugging the touristas to buy some fruit or candy or little clay sculptures of the ruins or some ancient god. Mitch was struck by one skinny kid, not more than twelve years old, carrying an old aluminum cooler around by a makeshift canvas strap looped over his shoulders, selling semi-cold sodas. The kid laughed with the other boys, and didn't seem to mind the pressing weight on his shoulders or being disdained by the excited tourists checking their cameras and crowding around their guide on the way in or being mobbed by the sweaty, bedraggled groups on their way out. Mitch wondered what the locals really thought about the touristas. He thought he knew human nature but there really didn't seem to be much resentment or jealousy in their attitudes. The obvious wealth of the visitors seemed more a source of bemused wonderment than of spite, and the locals whole attitude seemed to be one of amused tolerance. Mitch wondered if they just didn't know how expensive the cameras and clothes of the tourists were, how much "better off" these people were, or were they really wise enough to see that the so-called wealth of the modern world didn't really relate to them and that they were better off where they were. There was no clue on the faces of the men as they worked with machete and rake on the already well trimmed lawn or the faces of the women as they ate fruit and tended to the children in the shade of the near-by trees. The women and young girls were wearing the traditional Mayan dress, a one piece pullover, usually in white with colorful embroidery around the neck, sleeves and hem, which with their black hair, black eyes and proud bearing made them favorite subjects for the thirty-five millimeter cameras of the coffee-table anthropologists. Mitch turned his thoughts back to his own group as the Professor returned and gathered them around in the middle of the main plaza to begin his lecture tour.

"As many of you know," he began, "The site we are visiting today was a major religious and government center of the early classic period of Mayan culture, Mayan history being divided into three eras, the pre-classic, classic, and post-classic." Most of the grad students just nodded, being pretty familiar with Mayan history already, but some started taking notes as the professor went on about the subdivisions of each epoch, the periods divided by each advancement in culture such as the cultivation of maize or the formulation of the Mayan calendar. Each event marked the steady advance of a group of nomadic tribes a thousand years before Christ, to the settled, agricultural people with the time, energy, and inclination to realize great achievements in science and the arts, such as astronomy and architecture, a system of hieroglyphic writing, and an advanced system of political hegemony, to the tired and decadent nation swayed by Mexican Toltec influence and easily conquered by the Spanish Conquistadores of the late sixteen hundreds.

While Mitch wasn't listening to everything that Dr Comacho said, he was impressed by the respect shown to the Professor by the students, the one with the tape recorder standing next to and slightly behind him, holding out the machine so as not to miss even one of the master's words. Even the calm and easy-going Teo was listening intently and snapping pictures of everything with an old 110 camera he had hanging from his neck as he furiously scribbled what looked to Mitch like hieroglyphics in a battered, frayed notebook. The local guides seemed to know who he was and would nod in a dignified and respectful manner as he tactfully let them lead their groups of tourists on ahead. Guiding the tours was their livelihood, and Dr Comacho wanted to maintain the friendly working relationship that the expedition had enjoyed so far. After the last tour had gone on, the Professor led the group towards the foot of one of the main pyramids, constantly pointing things out to his fascinated entourage. Even though Mitch was interested in the Mayans, his short attention span and Elena's short pants did cause his mind to wander. He thought she looked really great today, kind of cute but sexy in her khaki safari shorts, with big pockets in front but snug across the back, hiking boots with white socks rolled down to her ankles, a yellow University t-shirt with no bra, and a khaki fishing-style cap with it's short brim pulled low over her eyes. Mitch noticed that she was standing on the edge of the group, not really listening to Dr Comacho, looking around on her own. As they walked to the base of the huge monument Mitch hung back and maneuvered himself around until he was next to Elena.

"I guess you've heard all this before,"

Mitch said, tilting his head towards where Dr Comacho had gathered the group and was going on about migrations and sacrifice and a bunch of gods and kings with indistinguishable names.

"Heard it?" Elena replied with a smile, "I teach it each year in freshman Anthropology!" She rolled her eyes and balled her fists on her hips in mock anger as an obviously surprised Mitch sputtered,

"You're a teacher? I thought, ah, I thought you . . ."

"That's right, Mr Male chauvinist," Elena interrupted, not really upset but with some measure of exasperation and more than a little pride in her voice, "And not just a teacher, but an associate professor, the youngest one in University history, and I expect to make full professor before too long, also." Then she half turned away, lowered her head to look flirtatiously at him from under the brim of her hat, laughed a sensual little laugh and said, "And you thought I was just another air-head with a pretty face and a great body, huh?" Before a confused but pleasantly excited Mitch could stammer out his protestations she shushed him with a finger to her lips and turned her attention back to her father, who was beginning another segment of his formal lecture.

"Now people, as you stand here in this magnificent plaza, you can get a feel for the awe that these tremendous structures must have struck in the hearts of the common people, who probably didn't live much differently than the villagers around here now, but who were ruled by a theocracy, or a group of warrior priests, who occupied these sacred areas and presided over the formal ceremonies and human sacrifices designed to appease the gods and insure success in agriculture. But also remember as you look at the dull gray and brown stone slabs around you that these were not their colors then. Remember that this was a vibrant, powerful civilization, in tune with the cycles of nature and of the heavens, and they were very much into color. The High Priest would appear at the door of the chamber on top of this pyramid," the Professor turned and pointed up the steep, high steps leading up the front of the monument, "Wearing a feathered headdress, brilliant gold and jade jewelry, including the ceremonial jade necklace that marked his high position, and a magnificent floor-length robe made entirely of thousands and thousands of hummingbird feathers. He would be surveying a scene of riotous color everywhere, from the brilliant robes of his fellow priests lining the plaza and the steps of the temple, to the simpler but still colorful clothes of the workers and ordinary people gathered there. The Steles you see around the perimeter of the plazas, each one symbolizing a period on their calendar, were painted a dark red or blue, and even the pyramid walls themselves were covered with plaster and painted the myriad colors of the jungle, leaning heavily towards red, blue, green, and yellow. Unfortunately the plaster didn't stand the test of time as well as the stone, so you will have to take my word for it and use your imagination." The Professor then smiled and said, "Now we will go to the top of this pyramid to study the priest's chamber. You will get a magnificent view of the entire area and maybe see some of the last vestiges of the color I have been describing inside the chamber, where it has been somewhat protected from the elements. Just keep in mind that whatever you see is upwards of fifteen hundred years old and shouldn't be toughed. Also," Dr Comacho turned back to the attentive little group and said kindly, "I know this is a steep climb, and if any of you are afraid of heights or just don't want to go, I'll understand. You can wait here and we will describe to you what we see, okay?" Of course no one in the group accepted Dr Comacho's invitation to wait. They looked around at each other, shaking their heads, some saying, "Let's go" and pointing up the staircase. Mitch was a little surprised because some of them didn't look too athletic to him, but he thought, "I guess if they're interested enough to come this far they aren't about to stop now." He looked up to see the Professor climb up a couple of steps, then turn and tell them,

"Now you all see this chain that was kindly put here by the government," he looked down and smiled at Teo, who was apparently taking a close-up picture of the chain, "No, Teo, it's not of Mayan origin," he went on as the grad students chuckled and Teo grinned sheepishly, "But we will use it today. I want one of you on each side of the chain, hold on to it tightly and follow me up the steps slowly. When we reach the top keep going to the back of the temple so the people behind you can get up, ok? Let's go!" With that the Professor turned and started up the stairs. As Mitch milled around waiting for his turn at the steps, he thought the Professor was making kind of a big deal out of the climb. These ruins were tall all right, maybe a little taller than a ten story building, but Mitch had been as high as thirty-seven stories working construction down in Miami. So he started to climb in a pretty nonchalant manner, sliding his hand over the chain as he went, joking with the people around him, grabbing Louis's leg ahead of him and just generally acting the fool for Elena. But about halfway up he found himself gripping the chain more tightly, not kidding around anymore, concentrating on the chain and the steps directly in front of him. Mitch noticed that no one else was saying much either, just purposely climbing up and up, many using their free hand to grab the step above them, making headway in a kind of vertical crawl. Mitch gained some instant respect for the ancient Mayan architects as he reflected, "Maybe ten stories just seems a lot higher in contrast to the flat jungle around here, or maybe it's these damn steps, but this is scary." The steps were tall, over two feet high, but narrow, maybe less than a foot wide on top. This, together with the steps steep angle going up the side of the pyramid, made it easy to get a feeling of vertigo, like you were going to topple over backward. That was the reason for the chain and Mitch made full use of it until he finally scrambled over the last step and stood up on a wide ledge or porch around the small temple that crowned the pyramid. The Professor put his hand on Mitch's shoulder as Mitch bent over to slap the dirt off his knees.

"Don't feel bad, Mitch," he said, "Almost everybody comes over the top like that." Mitch had to admit to himself that he didn't feel very macho right then, but as he looked around and took in the view it all seemed worth it. Seen from the top of one of the tallest pyramids the others could have been stone islands, rising from a green sea of surrounding and strangling vegetation, showing the effects of the elements and the years, but basically defying time and retaining the mysterious force of their silent and massive magnificence long after the people who conceived and constructed them were gone. The ones bordering the central plaza had been completely cleared, showing their layered construction and steep steps, the temple on top being a thick walled rectangular building with a square opening or entranceway and a stone comb, sort of like a wall of bas-relief on the top. Mitch was wondering what the function of the combs was when Dr Comacho started to address the group once again.

"As you can see by the number of pyramids," he lectured, "Their size and the distance between them, that this was a major center of the Classic period. Each temple is in honor of a different deity, for example the god of corn. Some archeologists believe that the carved and painted combs marked the temple of the individual gods, sort of like ancient billboards, but that's just a theory and they may be strictly decorative, we don't know. We do know that the people depended on agriculture to survive and that much of the religious practice focused on appeasing these gods and enlisting their help to insure good crops. This probably led to the Mayans developing their very accurate calendar, keeping track of the cycles of the crops, when to plant, etcetera, and possibly led to their interest in astronomy, studying the phases of the moon and the cycles of the stars. It may also have led to the general destruction of their civilization, when this and other great cities were all abandoned within a century." Mitch smiled to himself as he saw the graduate students start nodding and talking among themselves; a person couldn't travel very far in Central America, especially if he was at all interested in the ruins, without hearing about the great Mayan disappearance. It seems for some mysterious reason the Mayans elaborate system of culture and rule simply collapsed and the people left their great cities for the jungle to reclaim and migrated elsewhere in the region. It wasn't really the end of Mayan civilization, but it did mark the beginning of a long decline into periods of civil war, domination by Northern Mexican tribes, obscurity and mystery. Now anyone who had anything to do with the ruins, even just passing through as a tourist, had an opinion as to why the Mayans left. Mitch looked around and saw Elena examining the walls of the temple just inside the open entranceway, and started easing over there himself as the Professor elaborated on the theories and speculations.

"Now, the fact of the matter is that no one knows for sure why the Mayans migrated during those periods known as the Great Descent and the Lesser Descent. It is one of the great mysteries of archeology, and may never be solved to everyone's satisfaction." Dr Comacho paused for a moment, looked around him and smiled as he saw all the eager students, their young minds bursting with desire to learn the answer to the riddle. He continued, "To me, that is also one of the great pleasures of archeology, the anticipation of possibly unraveling an ancient mystery like this, the openness of the field to allow so many theories on the same matter. There are so many theories, and they run from the reasonable to the ridiculous; who can give me a reasonable one?" There was a fairly long moment of restrained silence before one of the grad students half raised his hand and said,

"Disease, an epidemic of some sort maybe." That broke the ice and the bold grad student smiled smugly as the Professor said "Good", and several others blurted out their examples. The Professor stopped them by raising his hands, palms out, finger up,

"Okay, I heard several good ones; crop failure, poisoned water supply, a drought or peasant revolt, he said. "All reasonable, and each with some evidence to support it, but all very difficult to prove." Dr Comacho made a fist and pumped his arm up and down as he looked around the semi-circle and said excitedly, "But that's what we're here for, right?" Mitch stepped up next to Elena as the little group excitedly shook hands, slapped each other on the back and babbled out their confidence.

"Your father definitely has a lot of charisma," Mitch said softly to her as they stood in the shadowy entranceway.

"He sure does, "Elena replied, smiling proudly, her dark eyes shining.

"Well, I think it runs in the family," Mitch said, leaning slightly in towards her, his hand braced against the cool stone of the temple wall. Elena gave him a quick, pleased look but then shushed him again as her father went on.   "Okay, now for an example of a ridiculous idea, there is the "aliens" theory. This 'theory' is based solely on speculation as to why or how the Mayans rose relatively quickly, in anthropological terms, and then supposedly disappeared even more quickly. The story goes that an alien, a visitor from another planet, crash-landed in the jungle and guided the backward Indians he found there to advanced civilization. Proponents of this theory state the fact that although the Mayans did not know the use of the wheel and did not have the arch incorporated into their architecture, they still achieved great advances in math, calendar making, astronomy, and obviously, monument building." Dr Comacho paused and looked all around, at the students and past them to review the bones of this once magnificent city, then resumed with a scowl, "That theory is not only ridiculous , it is insulting and probably racially motivated as well. As if the local people couldn't possibly achieve so much without outside help, and that they lost everything when the 'White God' left. That is not even true as we are discovering more and more about how pervasive Mayan influence was and how long it lasted. I personally think we ought to concentrate on the local population and not seek out or invent some out side influence." The little group was somewhat cowed by the intensity of the Professor's outburst but their innate curiosity won out as one of them asked,

"Excuse me, sir, but which theory do you feel is the most likely?"

"Well, it's not the spaceman theory," the Professor laughed, dispelling much of the tension. "Actually, I feel a combination of things, based on soil depletion, probably brought on the migrations. Remember the priests and rulers held absolute power by supposedly being good with the gods and doing the right things to ensure good harvests. Meanwhile the poor oppressed farmers were practicing the same slash and burn agriculture we still see today, and they eventually depleted all the soil, couldn't produce enough food for the growing population, and this led to a peasant revolt against the ruling priests, who in the eyes of the populace had failed in their duty. Having used up all the soil and toppled the system of government, the people simply moved on, but actually kept most of the essential ingredients of Mayan culture and eventually rose to periods of greatness again in other parts of the peninsula. That's one of my ideas on the subject but there is still much to learn, so now let's go inside the temple and perhaps we can see some color left on the frescos." With that he turned and walked past Mitch and Elena into the dark and musty interior of the temple. As the little knot of students and followers squeezed in Mitch and Elena shuffled out along the wall.

"Look at this," Elena said softly to Mitch,

shaking her head as the last of the students went by, "Graffiti, would you believe it? Hundreds of miles out in the jungle, a two thousand year old temple and these people have got to write their names on the walls? 'Umberto and Octavia, Julio and Maria, Jack and Kelly from Ohio'? Have these people no sense of history, no manners?" Mitch looked at the pitiful etchings, scratches left by people looking for a little piece of immortality, people who tried to cover up their insignificance in the face of the overwhelming span of time evidenced here by commemorating their presence and their "everlasting" love by writing their names on the wall of the ancient temple. Mitch shook his head and looked at Elena, so genuinely perplexed and upset by their petty acts. He could understand her anger but he wanted to lighten the mood so he said,

"Well, there's no excuse for what they did, but I think I could understand their intentions." He pause and smiled at Elena as she turned from the graffiti to give him a sharp look, "I mean, young love, alone in the face of all this history, marooned together in the heat of the jungle night . . . ". Elena's look turned slightly dubious as she tried to figure out if he was serious or not but before she could answer, Louis strolled by fanning his face with his hand.

"Whew," he said, looking sideways at Mitch and Elena, "It's getting pretty steamy in here." Elena flushed a deep red under the lighter red of the beginnings of a sunburn as Louis went on, "You better slow down, Mitch, or we're going to have to toss you into the 'Well of Souls' to cool you off. It's over there somewhere," he said, pointing out past one of the other tall monuments as they came out into the bright sunlight and moved to the side along the portico around the temple to give the Professor and the others room to emerge from the interior, "That's where we're headed next." Mitch stood to the side as the little party began to carefully go back down the steep steps, stared out towards where Louis had pointed and reflected,

"Damn, you can't see any part of it, even from up here. I wonder where the water comes from? Maybe a creek or stream down there somewhere?" Mitch knew that it could be rainwater or ground water coming up from the aquifer, "But as thick as that jungle is," he thought, "There could be a mighty river under the tree canopy and you would never know it." He also thought about how easy the jungle could swallow up something as insignificant as a person and resolved to either stay with somebody who knew where they were going or not go very far into the bush.

Later they were sitting on some benches in the shade outside the refreshment stand, drinking "jugos" and giving everyone a chance to use the facilities or just to cool off some before plunging into the air-conditioned museum. They had hiked the quarter mile or so (it was really difficult to judge distance when you couldn't see more than fifty feet in any direction) to the "Well of Souls", the sacrificial lake where the fanatical priests had thrown the bodies of young virgins, or sometimes the drugged but living victims, after ceremoniously sacrificing them to appease the gods. Dr Comacho had gone on about how human sacrifice wasn't typical of the Early Classic periods but was more an evidence of later Toltec influence, and that the "victims" actually saw themselves as "honorees" and went voluntarily, even happily, to their fate.

"Oh, yeah," thought Mitch, "Then why did they have to drug them?" Mitch wasn't very impressed by the well itself, though. It reminded him a lot of the sinkholes he had seen and swam in around Gainesville, Florida, only this one's steep, sheer walls precluded any swimming because once in, you wouldn't be able to get out again. Also the water in the sinkholes around Gainesville was usually gin-clear, being fed by underground streams, whereas the water here was clouded by the jungle run-off. Whatever evidence left of the dramatic events and high ceremonies that had occurred here was lost beneath the still, aqua water. So Mitch just stood around sweating and slapping mosquitoes, waiting for Dr Comacho, who was so intent that he didn't seem to notice either the heat or the bugs, to finish that section of his lecture, half listening to the Professor as he tried to think of a cool approach to try on Elena.

"Uh oh, watch it Teo, here comes the guard," Mitch said urgently in a loud half-whisper as they got up and walked towards Dr Comacho, who was standing in front of the entrance to the museum waving them over. The guard in question was a sleepy looking Mexican with a snappy officer's cap, a polished black leather belt and holster covering up his sidearm, and a good start on a substantial belly befitting a man of his authority stretching his neatly pressed light blue uniform shirt across his mid-section. He was moving in their direction mostly to get out of the way of the eager grad students coming to join the Professor at the door as Mitch continued, "Damn, Teo, how did they know that you are an internationally famous antiquities thief? Come on Louis, help me hide him!" A confused Teo started to respond as Mitch and Louis stepped shoulder to shoulder in front of him, their best "hard-guy" looks on their faces, but a smiling Elena came to his rescue first, saying,

"Come on, Mitch, quit fooling around. Besides," she said, as Teo laughed and grabbed the guys by their shoulders, stuck his head in between theirs and said, 'You'll never take me alive!', "Museum security isn't always a joke, you know. As a matter of fact, just the week before my father and I left the capitol one of the most famous museums was robbed by a highly skilled and professional gang of thieves. They got away with many well known and valuable pieces."

"But wait a minute," interjected Louis, "If the pieces are well known, how can the thieves sell them or the buyer display them?"

"Well, unfortunately Louis," replied Elena, "There are collectors out there who don't care if they can display the artifacts or how they got them. They just want to possess them, to have the best collection or whatever. I don't understand them myself. But it's not impossible that one of these collectors hired the thieves specifically for that job, to get the artifacts he wanted."

"Pretty heavy stuff," muttered Mitch as they followed Dr Comacho into the cool, dimly lit interior of the museum. The display area was a long, rectangular room, with two rows of wood and glass display cases back to back down the center and a series of dioramas built into recesses of the walls with glass windows facing inside. Most of the light was coming from the soft, sterile fluorescent lights illuminating the display cases and artfully hidden the ceilings and backgrounds of the dioramas showing scenes of Mayan life and history. The subdued lighting and air-conditioning, designed to keep a constant temperature on the relics, had an effect on people as well as everyone finished shuffling for position and turning pages in their notebooks and just stood quietly around the Professor where he had stopped at the head of the row of display cases.

"Now," the Professor began in a low but clear voice, "Some of the artifacts you see here are not the real ones. They are copies, not so much fakes as substitutes for the real relics, which have been removed to the capitol for safe-keeping, or supposed safe-keeping." His last comment seemed to be a reference to the robbery that Elena had just mentioned. "But," Dr Comacho continued, "The copies have been so meticulously crafted that only an expert would be able to tell that they are not genuine. And besides, they do accurately represent the aspects of Mayan theory and state of knowledge we have. Okay, so now let us begin. We will start on the right and move completely around the room, and I will give a brief description of what we are viewing and answer any questions, yes?" With that he started along the wall followed by his intent disciples. Again Mitch hung back towards the rear of the group, partly because although he was interested in Mayan history in general, he didn't want to get in the way of any of the "true believers", people like Teo and the grad students, people who were likely to make the study of Mayans a big part of their lives, not just a side street on the way to somewhere else like he was, and partly because that's where Elena was, amusing herself by trying to pick out the fake artifacts in the displays. But unfortunately for Mitch the hushed atmosphere in the room and the acoustic properties of the glass walls made even the softest voice carry to all corners of the room, and Mitch was too inhibited to initiate any verbal banter, so he had to content himself with glances, smiles, and occasional closeness as they both leaned over the same display case, while listening to Dr Comacho's lecture. The Professor was a good lecturer, commanding everyone's attention in such a way as to never have to raise his voice, where every inflection of his voice or nuance of gesture was noted as intended. To Mitch it seemed that they were getting too bogged down in minutia and detail but his interest was renewed by the centerpiece of the exhibit, a facsimile of a royal tomb. Taking up the whole back wall of the museum, the tomb consisted of a sunken chamber about twenty feet long by ten feet wide, with smaller ancillary cubicles along one side. As Mitch waited his turn to stand on the single step that allowed the viewer to look down into the ersatz pit through the glass wall, the Professor was telling the group how this represented the final resting place of a powerful king or ruler-priest. Dr Comacho related how the royal deceased was surrounded by supplies, food, and belongings to take with him, not the least of which were his favorite slaves and wives, who were buried with him in the small cubicles adjacent to his chamber. They were considered his belongings and part of his valuables, so they were entombed with him, after being ceremoniously sacrificed if they were lucky, or buried alive if they weren't. But when Mitch finally stepped up and looked into the chamber, he could see what would really be considered the king's valuables by the modern world. For there on the floor of the burial chamber lay an ordinary human skeleton wearing the most extraordinary and elaborate collection of jade and gold jewelry that Mitch had ever seen. On each ankle and wrist he wore bracelets made out of little rectangles of solid jade perhaps an inch long and half an inch wide, some carved to look like human skulls, perhaps representing enemies killed in battle or sacrifice, all tied together with gold strands and little beads of jade and semi-precious stones. On his skull rested a death mask consisting of many pieces of flat and artful jade molded together to rise and fall with the contours of his face and topped off by magnificent ear-flares, sort of large, elaborate earrings, usually rising up alongside the temples instead of hanging down, attached to the death mask with intricate little clasps of solid gold. Around his neck he had an immense jade and gold necklace, similar to his bracelets but much larger. The segments of jade, which were held together by finely filigreed gold wire, were each about the size of a candy bar, three to four inches long, one inch and a half to two inches wide and about an inch thick. The necklace came around both sides of the skeleton's neck, hanging in a macabre way down between each rib, before meeting near the sternum and continuing along for several segments to his waist. Now the segments were lying haphazardly along the dead ruler's vertebrae, proving his lack of divinity once and for all. But even Mitch, who didn't wear any jewelry at all, not a necklace, ring, or even a wristwatch, could understand how people could want to possess such a treasure. "There are people in Miami who would kill for just one of those pieces," Mitch thought cynically, "Those must not be real, or they would have more than just one lazy guard." Whether the jewelry was real or not, it still made for an impressive exhibit, and it definitely had the desired effect on the little group following Dr Comacho. They lingered there longer than anywhere else, talking excitedly among themselves, pointing out certain exquisite workings of the jade or pottery, or even just features of the tomb. There were more exhibits to see in the museum, and the Professor went on with his lecture, with his people dutifully following along, but it was clear their minds were still on the king's tomb. Their excitement was only heightened when the Professor gathered them together once again at the end of the tour and said,

"Now, you have all had a chance to see some of the goals of our expedition, some of the rewards of our profession." He paused and looked around at the little knot of excited faces circled around him, "And I don't mean the jade or gold, but the knowledge gained, the little pieces of information dug so painstakingly out of the past by our colleagues that came before us. Of course, finding a royal burial chamber would be the ultimate, meaning the area was a major, important center." He paused while the fired up and confident students smiled and nodded, shuffling around and slapping each other on the back, "But remember," he cautioned, "Today you have seen some of the results and goals of archeology, but starting tomorrow, you will see some of the other side, the long hours, tough conditions, and hard work." Dr Comacho's stern words didn't seem to dampen anyone's spirit though, as they set out eagerly down the trail to return to camp and begin working. Mitch didn't know what to expect; he thought about the ride, the heat, the bugs, and the jungle, but he also thought of Elena, his growing friendship with Teo and Louis, and he had to admit that it had been pretty interesting so far. He figured he would stick around for a little while at least.

Chapter Four: The Monkey Hunt

"Rice and beans, rice and beans, that's all we ever eat anymore," moaned Louis.

"Well," said Teo, "You've got to pay your dues in order to learn something."

"Hey, well, I've learned that archeology is hard work," replied Mitch.

"Not all work, eh Mitch?" smiled Louis, "We see the way you try to spend time with Elena."

"Better than looking at you two uglies," retorted Mitch.

"Yeah, you're lucky," said Teo, "We have to make do on rice and beans while you can live on love."

"Well, the new supplies are supposed to

arrive soon," laughed Mitch.

"Maybe," Louis came back, "We haven't seen them yet."   "Don't worry, they'll get here," said Mitch. But he didn't feel as confident as he sounded. He had seen the worried look in Elena's eyes all week. The expedition had operated on a shoestring from the beginning and Dr Comacho spent more and more of his time in Tovalado, the nearest town of any size, trying to get the government to come up with more money. This left Elena in charge a lot and Mitch was worried about her working too hard. He walked over to her tent in the cool evening air and found her sitting at her table working on the books.

"Oh, hi, Mitch," Elena said as she looked up smiling, "How   are you?"

"I'm fine." replied Mitch, "The question is, why are you still working? You need your rest."

Elena put down her pencil and sat back in her canvas chair, rubbing the back of her neck with one hand while motioning to Mitch to come in and sit on her footlocker with the other. Elena wondered about Mitch as she watched him come in and sit on the edge of the locker. For the few weeks that they had been down there she had been watching him, but she couldn't figure him out. Tall and a little on the lean side, he was strong, could work hard and obviously kept his body in good shape. He had sandy brown hair, large brown eyes and a bushy mustache that framed his willing smile, and that smile, along with his easy-going manner and dry humor made him an easy guy to like and to get along with. Elena saw the students and workers kind of naturally gravitate to him as a leader as the work of hacking out the jungle and setting up their permanent base camp went on and as her father gave Mitch more and more responsibility for running the work force. And Mitch didn't seem to be on the self destructive trip that a lot of the older gringo backpackers, especially ones down for the second or third time, seemed to be on with drugs, alcohol, or cheap local women. But even though Mitch appeared to be a straightforward guy, Elena felt that there was something more there, something he didn't show as readily. There was an intensity in those brown eyes that betrayed his mellow persona, in spite of his jokes and his jeans and his couple of beers in the evening with the guys. Elena had seen him a few times staring into the fire or looking vacantly off into the jungle. If she asked him what he was thinking about he would say, "Nothing," and then talk about the work, or camp scuttlebutt, or something like that. "Oh, well," thought Elena, "I wonder if he's running from something or looking for something?" She looked at his friendly, worried face and replied, "I've got to figure out how to save money on supplies." She sighed deeply, "We're almost broke and poor Papa has to humble himself and practically beg the government just to get them to live up to their pledges." She shifted her chair around slightly to face him more directly, "Did you notice that we had to let go three of the local workers, and a couple of students have also left?" she asked.

"Yeah," he replied, "Maybe they got sick of rice and beans." Mitch saw the look of pain and frustration on Elena's face and was immediately sorry he had said it. "Look, I'm sorry," he said, putting his arm around her shoulder to comfort her, "Maybe we can get some fresh meat by hunting around here."

Elena's face brightened, then fell, "That would be great, but I don't think the government would allow it," she sighed resignedly.

"They will if they don't know about it," grinned Mitch. He was kind of surprised to hear his own words, because he was certainly no poacher, but looking down into Elena's worried eyes, he convinced himself that this was a special case.   "Oh, Mitch, you are so nice," Elena said as she sagged against him. He squeezed her hand and then held her while all the anger, worry, and frustration came out and she sobbed quietly in his arms.

"Don't worry," he said, "Teo, Louis and I will go out tomorrow and get us some fresh meat. Everything will be all right." She looked up at him and he saw those big brown eyes and he kissed her. She seemed a little surprised but she didn't pull away. They stayed like that for a long moment, holding each other, looking into each others eyes. Finally Mitch said, "You're tired." He released her from his arms. "Get some rest, I'll see you tomorrow." He left her tent and stepped into the cool night air. He was pleased to see her lantern go out as he was walking to his tent, adding his whistle to the wild sounds of the jungle all around him.

*   *   *

      Mitch rubbed his eyes trying to wake up and pulled his coat tighter against the chill of the pre-dawn air. He and Louis and Teo were walking quietly down the path to the far side of the campground, Where Herman and Perez, two of the local workers who had been with them since the beginning, were to meet them. Perez had claimed to have a hunting rifle and they both knew the surrounding jungle the way only someone who lived there can. Perez had a rifle, all right, an ancient twenty-two bolt action that used to have a clip but was now a single – shot. That and a handful of old cartridges and Mitch's Buck knife would be their equipment. Louis yawned extravagantly and said, "All right, we are all here, what are we going to hunt?

Tapir? Rabbit? Monkeys?"

"Monkeys,?" asked Teo, incredulous,
"I'm not eating monkey!"

"Aw, come on, Teo," replied Mitch, "It's
all going into a stew anyway. Let's just start out
and bag the first thing we see."

"Right," said Perez as he set out down a
trail used only by locals, "This is a meat hunt
and we shall get some."

The heavy, earthy aroma of the thick
vegetation in the moist early morning air, the
hushed voices of his friends as they shuffled
along in the cathedral-like atmosphere caused
by the gray, luminous light of dawn streaming
through the jungle canopy, or just the feeling of
being out and about first, before the rest of the
world woke up, caused Mitch to reminisce
about the hunting and fishing trips his old man
used to take him and his brothers on back in
Fort Lauderdale. He marveled at the courage of
the man, loading up his Fifty-three Chevy with
his three boys, one dog, and whatever
neighborhood kids could get their hands on a
twenty-two or even a BB gun and taking them
out on the coral and dirt roads west of town.

He would pull off State Road Eighty-four and
cross the Eighty-four canal on an old, rickety
wooden bridge, drive a way down the roads
laid in for housing projects that hadn't been
built yet, park the car, send the dog off into the
bushes and let the hunters fan out across the
road, walking along and shooting at anything
the dog could chase out of the bushes or
anything spotted in the canal or in the trees.
Mitch winced a little when he remembered the
day he had accidentally shot the dog. The dog
hadn't been seriously hurt, the twenty-two
short that Mitch was using barely penetrating
the hard cartilage of the dog's nose where it
had hit, and although it really wasn't Mitch's
fault, the dog having gone for a wounded rabbit
at the same moment that Mitch was trying to
administer the coup-de grace, Mitch had been
very upset. He had cried and yelled, and swore
off hunting forever, saying he never wanted to
touch a gun again. But his old man was very
understanding, telling him that these things
happened in life, that the dog would forget it
and so should he. And sure enough Mitch did
eventually get over it but he also remembered

that although his father carried a Twenty-two revolver, he almost never shot anything, often spotting a rabbit or something hiding in the bushes and not saying anything, just letting his gang of little killers walk on by. Mitch could understand his father's attitude better as he got older, preferring to live and let live, but this was a special case, and there really wasn't any bad karma or anything attached to hunting if you did it out of necessity.

The Florida of Mitch's youth was a great place for a sportsman or a kid to live. It was possible to fight a hundred pound Tarpon in the surf in the morning and catch Large-mouth Bass in the old bombing range west of town in the afternoon. Or try your hand at deer or hog hunting in the Everglades, or air-boating for frogs and alligators, or maybe trolling for Dolphin offshore or snorkeling for "Bugs", as lobsters were called. But Mitch shook his head sadly as he remembered how all the roads eventually got paved, how all the housing projects were built and all the houses sold, begetting more projects to the west of them, all the way out to State Road Twenty-seven, the eastern boundary of the Everglades. How the New River went from crystal clear to brown, lined with boats of every description, the canals all succumbing to seawalls and marinas jammed with live-aboards. The urban, or more accurately, suburban sprawl had spread out and smothered both the physical territory and the lifestyle that Mitch loved so much. That was one of the reasons Mitch had come to Central America in the first place. He loved it's frontier atmosphere, it's not being over developed, it's raw, natural beauty. Now he was here, seeing that nature wasn't in retreat everywhere, and he felt good, breathing in the smooth, cool morning air and feeling the smooth, hard outline of the twenty-two rifle cradled in his arms. "Now this was getting involved in the local color," thought Mitch as he hiked behind Perez, scanning the high branches of the jungle canopy above them for monkeys. He didn't particularly want to eat monkey meat either but he was pretty tired of rice and beans. It was strange the indigenous people ate mostly carbohydrates when the rain forest around them was full of protein. The people ate eggs and chicken, and fish and some turtle over on the coast sometimes but mostly they ate rice, beans, or yucca. Yucca was the root of a bush and sort of resembled candied yams when cooked but tasted a lot like paste. "Maybe that's why the people were generally smaller in stature than North Americans," he mused as he picked his way over the roots and rocks on the trail. It didn't mean they weren't strong, though. Mitch had come to greatly admire and respect Perez and Herman, especially after seeing them work all day without complaining. The two of them could get out there with machetes and cut the grass in the entire compound by hand just as neatly and nearly as quickly as a power lawnmower. The machete is the campesino's favorite, most constant, and most useful tool. They preferred the long blades, three feet long, and they kept them razor sharp. The men carried them almost constantly from the time they were boys and could do anything with them, from opening a coconut for a drink, to cutting grass, to clearing the trail as they were doing now. The machetes were made of steel and their owners used a regular file to sharpen them. As sharpness was desired most the guys were continually fussing with their blades, running the file over the edge. But the machetes were expensive and would not be thrown away until they broke, so many were of varying thickness, from a full sized four or five inches wide, to saber-like blades barely an inch wide. Both Perez and Herman had fairly new, wide blades, but they weren't cutting too much because there already was a faint trail and they didn't want to make too much noise.

Mitch found that hunting in the jungle wasn't so easy as he had thought it would be. True, there were a lot of animals in the brush and the guys could hear them every once in a while scurrying away, but there was a lot of cover, too. Mitch was chosen to handle the rifle and he did manage to hit a monkey cleanly and it fell, dying before it hit the ground. Even so, it took most of a half an hour to find the carcass in the tangled weeds. Teo got stung by some kind of insect and was complaining constantly about monkey meat and what a problem it was to get.

"Oh,come on, Teo," laughed Louis, "You'll probably eat more than anybody."

"No way,"snorted Teo, "I like rice and beans . . .hey, what's that?" Teo pointed towards a vine covered pile of rocks and Mitch spotted what he was pointing at. It was a Capi Bara, sort of a large rat, a muskrat or something, just ambling around the pile. Mitch raised the gun and fired. He heard the dull thud of a bullet striking flesh and he knew he hit it but the big rodent took off. Mitch dug in his pocket for another round for the twenty-two, while Teo, Louis, Herman, and Perez ran on opposite sides of the pile of rocks to try and keep it in sight. Mitch had just gotten the next bullet chambered when suddenly Perez and Herman burst out of the bush yelling,

"Madre Dios, El Tigre, El Tigre!"

"Oh my God," thought Mitch, "A Jaguar...where are Teo and Louis?" Mitch ran over to the side of the mound, the old twenty – two at the ready. The Jaguar was definitely the King of the Jungle in the Western Hemisphere. More closely resembling a leopard than a lion or a tiger, just as agile as a leopard but much larger, the full grown cat could be as much as eight feet long and weigh over three hundred pounds. Mitch remembered the nasty, almost evil look that blazed in the yellow-gold eyes of the big male at Miami's Metro Zoo as he stared steadily at the people edging by, nervously eyeing the distance across the moat between him and them. Mitch wasn't looking forward to seeing one without a moat at all. "Shit, this thing will only piss him off," worried Mitch as he held the rifle. Beyond the pile of rocks were more mounds, covered with vines and vegetation and pock-marked with shallow holes and dark depressions. Mitch could hear the big cat growling and see the brush shaking where he was but Mitch couldn't see him for a clear shot. Then he spotted Teo half-way up a tree.

"You all right, Teo?" yelled Mitch.

"Yeah, so far," shouted back Teo, hanging on for dear life, "But Louis is in trouble over there." He pointed to a large mound just above where the cat was growling. Mitch crept carefully over to the other side of the mound until he could see Louis crunching down behind a large rock. He scanned the low brush between the mounds, hoping to see some movement that would show him more precisely where the animal was, or maybe a route that Louis could use to come around the mound and back with them. He still couldn't see the beast and now it was quiet except for an occasional low growl, but he knew that the big cat was somewhere just across from Louis. Mitch knew that the twenty-two would not stop the big beast in a charge. Mitch's breath was coming in short gasps as drops of sweat rolled down into his eyes and his knuckles turned white from gripping the stock of the single –shot rifle. He hoped to get everybody out of there without shooting if he could and he was trying to think of a way to pull it off when suddenly Louis saw Mitch. Louis was as white as a ghost, nearly panic- stricken as he gripped the vines on the side of the rock. When he saw Mitch his eyes got as wide as plates and he jumped up and started running towards him. "No, no," yelled Mitch as he jumped to his feet, "Stay there, stay down!" But it was too late. As Louis got to the bottom of the mound Mitch saw a flash of yellow out of the corner of his eye as the jaguar charged. He raised the twenty-two and fired in desperation just as he saw Louis stumble and fall into a hole between two large rocks, the surprised jaguar screaming his rage and biting at the wound on his back, crouching right over the hole that Louis was lying in. Mitch ran forward a couple of steps, reloading frantically, then aimed carefully for the ear of the big cat, snapping off the round quickly but on target. The king of the jungle leapt twenty feet straight up and came down slashing and tearing at the vegetation with his razor sharp claws as he rolled and roared in pain and anger. Mitch reloaded and fired three more times, aiming for the head each time before the jaguar finally lay still, majestic even in death. The whole jungle was eerily quiet, as if it was waiting to see if this really was the end. Mitch stood there shivering for a minute and then ran to meet Teo rushing over to where Louis had disappeared. They got down on their bellies and looked into the depression. There was Louis, huddled into as small a ball as he could make of himself. He looked up into his friend's worried faces,

"Is it over? Is everyone ok?"

"Whew," laughed Teo, "We are, how about you?" "I'm ok but I'm going to have to change my underwear," Louis said somewhat giddily. Mitch and Teo gave him a hand up as all the tension and anxiety were released in a burst of wild laughter. Perez and Herman approached carefully. "Did you get him, Senor?" they asked.

"Yeah, I think so," answered Mitch, reloading again, "Let's go see." The jaguar lay on its side, unmoving as Mitch prodded it with the rifle barrel. "I guess it's dead, all right," he said. He saw the little trickle of blood coming out of a small hole behind the big cat's ear. "I didn't think that one of these little twenty-two's would kill one of those bastards!"

"Yes, God was certainly with us today," Herman said, crossing himself reverently.

"Well, I'm glad that it did and He was," put in Louis, sitting down on a little mound, his face pale and drained from the shock setting in.

"Yeah, I guess we were lucky," said Teo, examining the slashes in the ground, Look how close he came to you; there are scratches just above where you were in there." Mitch and Louis came over to where Teo was pointing at the side of the crevice.

"Wait a minute," said Mitch, "These over here aren't scratches; here, take a look Teo." Teo leaned down into the crack and ran his hands over the side of the rock.

"Hey, these are hieroglyphs! These mounds could be undiscovered pyramids . . . I've got to get down there," he shouted, all fired up.

"Hey, wait a minute," yelled Louis as Teo started to climb down into the crack, "What about the jaguar's mate? It might still be around here somewhere." Teo stopped in his tracks.   "You think so?" he asked Mitch.

"Well, I don't know, but what about the one we do have here?" asked Mitch.

"No problem, Senor," replied Perez, "This was indeed a lucky hunt, since El Tigre was hit mostly in the head, because we can sell the pelt in town and make lots of money for supplies."

"Wait a second," asked Mitch, "Isn't that illegal? I mean, aren't jaguars a protected species? Can we sell it?"

"How much money are we talking about?" broke in Louis, "I mean the cat is already dead and I don't feel sorry for him at all."

"Yes, but we don't want to get into any trouble with the authorities," stated Teo.

"Don't worry, you guys," said Herman, "I know a guy who won't ask questions and this could be good for weeks of good provisions, and of course, rice and beans."

"Ok," said Mitch, "Since this whole hunt is not exactly legal, but our motives were good, and since it would be a sin to just let the pelt rot, I say take it. Agreed?" Everyone nodded their assent. "I'll take Perez and Herman into town and let them handle the sale, ok? But for now let's pack it in, I've had enough excitement for one day." They all laughed in agreement.

"Well, I'm going to pick up a few shards while Perez is skinning the cat, okay?" asked

Teo.

"Sure, but be careful," replied Mitch.

Chapter Five: Discovery

A few nights later they were all sitting
around in the kitchen tent, drinking coffee and

savoring the memory of the evening meal. Tonight had been ham and boiled potatoes purchased with jaguar skin money. Even the monkey and capi bara stew had tasted fairly good after weeks of a bland diet. Herman had done well in town on the pelt and Elena had stretched every peso to the limit in shopping for supplies. Elena had told her father about the hunt and about the big cat; while he said he probably wouldn't have approved it beforehand, he could understand their motives and was pleased with the way it had turned out. He was talking now about his favorite subject; the ruins and the expedition's work.

"Oh, that was good," he said to Elena, complimenting her on dinner while he poured himself a shot of tequila in a camp cup, "I'm proud of you, my daughter, for the way you are handling the responsibility around here. The hunt should have been my decision, but I wasn't here."

"No, Father," she replied, pointedly ignoring the cup in his hand, "You were doing what you have to do to keep the project going and so was I. I know you would rather be on the dig working than in town trying to raise funds."

"Excuse me, sir," broke in Louis, "But how is it going, anyway?"

"What do you mean," answered the Professor, "The dig or the fund-raising?"

"Well, both I guess," replied Louis.

"Okay," said the Professor, "The problem is that they are tied together. We have been doing good, solid work here, basic research that has contributed to the general knowledge of Mayan culture, but nothing spectacular, no breakthroughs like a tomb that hasn't been robbed to help sell the project to the government or perhaps raise the interest of some private investors. So, raising money is hard and I have less time to be in the field where I belong." While this exchange was taking place between Louis and Dr Comacho, Teo was sitting in front of the lantern, holding some of the shards he had found on the monkey hunt up to the light.

"What have you got there, Teo," the Professor asked, ever curious, "Let me see one."

"Oh, they're just some pieces of pottery

I found where we got the jaguar," answered Teo. The Professor looked the pieces over carefully in the light.

"Wait a minute," he muttered as he examined a large shard, his face becoming agitated. His eyes grew bigger with each piece examined and his voice betrayed his excitement when he asked, "Can you find this place again?"

"I don't know," Teo responded, looking over to Mitch sitting to his left, "Mitch, how about you?"

"I'm not sure either, but I imagine Perez could find it again," replied Mitch, "Why, what's up?"

"He better find it!" the professor practically shouted, jumping up out of his camp chair, "Because unless I'm wrong these are shards from burial pottery, royal burial pottery! You guys may have found our breakthrough; a tomb must be around there somewhere. If we can find an undisturbed burial chamber it will put this project on the map!" Everyone was standing now and Elena ran into her father's arms. "All right, let's not get too excited," said the Professor, obviously excited, "We still have to find it. Let's get some sleep now and check it out in the morning, okay?" The fired up little group reluctantly broke up, talking excitedly about Teo's find as they headed for their tents.

*　　　　　*　　　　　*

"Jesus, I'm getting used to this dawn patrol stuff," thought Mitch as he blew into his cupped hands against the pre-dawn chill. The Professor had gotten them all up early, confessing that he hadn't been able to sleep. Now they all stood at the head of the small trail leading into the jungle. Perez and Herman, Perez with the reliable old twenty-two rifle, a couple of grad students ready to work, talking with Teo about the vine-covered mounds, Louis and Mitch, Elena and Dr Comacho. Dr Comacho gathered them all together.

"Listen," he paused and looked around the circle, making eye contact with each person, "If we find what I hope we will, we must keep it secret as much as we can. Mayan kings were buried with a lot of their valuables, gold, silver, beautifully worked jade, you've all seen it in the museum and you know how valuable it is. We don't want the word to get out until we are ready, right? Ok then, let's go!" Perez didn't have much trouble finding the place again, pointing out the places where they had gotten the monkey and where they had first seen the Capi Bara. Louis gave a spirited recital of the battle with the Jaguar as they made their way along the muddy, humid trail. The graduate students were enthralled and kept looking over their shoulders into the dense vegetation surrounding them, but the Professor hardly listened. He was constantly surveying his surroundings, sometimes going off the trail to check on some rocks or something. After about an hour of hiking, it had seemed much farther during the monkey hunt, they came upon the clearing with the mounds. Dr Comacho climbed immediately into the crack where Louis had hidden from the big cat.

"Be careful, Papa," Elena said anxiously. "Mitch, go down there with him," she asked imploringly. Mitch was about to crawl in when the Professor came backing out.

"Never mind," he said excitedly, "The way is blocked about ten feet back, but the signs look good." Mitch thought he had never seen the Professor look better, standing there all muddy and dirty, disheveled, with bits of leaves and sand in his hair, clutching some shards he had found in the cave. "There must have been an earthquake here sometime to shift those stones like that," he said to Teo, pointing down the seam of the depression, "We'll have to get some equipment up here, and some help."

"Do you think we should set up base camp out here?" asked Elena.

"Not just yet," replied her father, "We'll set up a secondary camp here for now."

"It's too bad the earthquake had to block our way," said Teo, shaking his head at the size of the stones to be moved,

"No, Teo," answered the Professor, putting his arm on Teo's shoulder, "Without the quake those shards would probably never have come to light, so nothing is all bad."

"You are right, Papa," put in Elena, smiling," now the government bureaucrats will have to open the purse strings a little."

"Let's hope so, daughter," replied Dr Comacho, "Let's hope so."

*   *   *

The dig turned out to be a major project. Clearing the jungle away was by itself a herculean task, involving everyone and taking nearly two weeks. In the first place, although the new dig couldn't have been more than a mile from the base camp, it was a mile down a slippery, narrow, muddy trail through the swelteringly hot and humid, insect filled jungle. Every piece of equipment, large or small, had to be carried by hand to the site. If you were carrying something large and heavy, like a block and tackle, it could become an ordeal of strained muscles, bruises, and insect bites. If one partner slipped, as happened quite often on the uneven trail, the full weight of the piece would fall on the partner remaining upright, causing him to drop his end too, but usually not before it bruised or nicked him somewhere. And if some kind of biting insect found you during a tricky section of the trail, you had to

let him feast until you came to a smoother part
of the trail when you could put down your
burden and belatedly squash the little son-of —
a-bitch. And the first impression of a large
clearing one got when coming upon the group
of mounds in the otherwise dense vegetation
of the tropical rain forest was a false
impression. Actually it wasn't a clearing,
because although the height and stony
composition of the pyramids had prevented the
largest trees from reclaiming the area, the
mounds themselves were covered by smaller
trees, their roots growing into the cracks
between the stones, slowly breaking the large
stones down to a pile of smaller ones, with
small plants and vines covering the resultant
rubble. And the area between the mounds was
thick with thin, sparse trees and squat, leafy
bushes and cacti and vines and whatever else.
But fortunately this smaller flora proved no
match for Perez and Herman and their
machetes. Even Elena and her father were out
with machete, pick, and shovel. But it was clear
that the find was an important one. It was a
collection of pyramids smaller than the ones

near base camp but symmetrically arranged and covered with carvings on those walls that were left undamaged by the earthquake. Mitch had looked at those carvings on the gray stone blocks many times during those weeks. He remembered from the Professor's tour of the main pyramids that they weren't gray then, but painted in the myriad bright colors of a hummingbird feather cape. Mitch would look around and try to get a feel of what it was like back then. Were the Mayans always so stern and fierce as they were often depicted? Was this a sterile place of worship or a viable, active social center? Were singing and laughing heard in the plaza? Were lover's rendezvous made in the side alleys between the monuments or did the courtyards echo only to the stern, dry lectures of the high priests or the measured tramp of the soldier's sandals? Mitch had often run his hand over the profile and feathered headdress of the soldier, or god?, or priest?, carved on one of the steles, a kind of mini-monument about four to six feet tall or sometimes round that were found lining the plaza. Dr Comacho couldn't wait and had cleaned this one up as soon as it was discovered. Mitch looked often at the fine detail of the man's face, the hieroglyphs, and wondered what these people were trying to say, what message they were trying to pass down through the years to us. "Oh, well, I guess I've been bitten by the archeology bug," mused Mitch, "And why not? I've been bitten by every other kind of bug in this damn jungle." Even Mitch could see that their new dig was an important one, and the Professor and Elena were all excited, but it was clear that it was an important find to everyone except the government bureaucrats, though. They had listened to the Professor's enthusiastic description of the dig but had remained unmoved. They said they couldn't approve any more money for the project until the artifacts that were found had been sent back to the capitol for study. But the Professor was too engrossed to stop now. When he returned to the base camp from his latest trip he looked depressed, even deranged. He barely said hello to Elena, pausing only to give her a dry kiss on the cheek before going to his tent. Mitch couldn't believe the change in the man in the last few weeks. When they had first started on the new dig he had taken firm control and ran the whole thing with military precision. He had shed the "professor" image early on and stood sun-burned and sweaty in his undershirt, but in on everything, encouraging everyone by word and example. He was always the scholar, though, getting excited by each find, each little piece of ancient debris, running to show Elena where she sat in the shade of a tent flap inventorying the dig. His eyes would be as wide as a little boy's as he held each piece and told her, "I'll send a letter to Montoya about this, it will really give him something to think about, things about other archeologists and their theories." And Mitch could see that Elena was so proud of her father at that time, and why not, Mitch thought. He admired the Professor too, for the Professor was a man with a mission in life and he was hard at work at completing a dream. But each trip to town, each bout with the bureaucracy seemed to take a little more out of him. Maybe being so near the grandeur of the Mayan kings on the one hand, and having to deal with the pettiness of today's rulers on the other really bothered him. Even physically, he seemed to have shrunk, his shoulders slumped and peeling as his sunburn wore off as he spent more and more time either in town or in his tent. His hair actually seemed to thin as his eyes sank back in his head and the dark circles grew beneath them. "I knew the man lived by these ruins," thought Mitch," but I didn't think he could die by them." Just then Elena appeared at Mitch's tent, crying.

"Óh, Mitch," she said between sobs, "Papa is at the dinner tent and he's drunk!"

"Ok, I'll see what I can do," said Mitch while heading out the tent flap, "Don't worry, I'll talk to him"

Mitch came upon a tense and depressed group of people in the mess tent. There was Dr Comacho standing at the head of the table, loudly haranguing the poor graduate students and workers with a tin cup of tequila waving wildly in his hand. Mitch could see through the mosquito netting as he approached the people sitting in tight little groups, uncomfortable and embarrassed. These were the Professor's friends, co-workers, and students, all people who respected him greatly, and it hurt them to see him this way. And yet they could feel his anguish as surely as he did. They felt it in the blisters on their hands, the dirt under their fingernails, the sunburn peeling off their shoulders, the insect bites on their ankles and legs. "If a government official were to show up now, these people might revive the Mayan custom of human sacrifice," thought Mitch as he pushed aside the tent flap and stepped in to confront Dr Comacho.

"Ah, Mitch, my gringo stalwart," shouted the Professor with an ugly little attempt at a smile on his reddened face, "Another man whose hard work will be for nothing, nothing because of money, filthy lucre, trashy little colored pieces of paper!"

"Oh, come on now, Doc," said Mitch as he sat on the table next to the Professor, "We have done some fine work here, look at all we have discovered already." Dr Comacho's eyes blazed briefly as Mitch spoke.

"By God, you're right, we have, we've done great work, we have some amazing artifacts," then he sagged back on the table by Mitch, chugged his tequila and said bitterly, "That's the irony of the whole thing, my good gringo friend, that we have priceless artifacts here, jade, pottery, hieroglyphs, and I can't get a peso from the government to put together an exhibit." Mitch spoke up as the Professor sighed, saying,

"Maybe this is too American, but why don't you just sell some artifacts; they have to be worth something on the market." Dr Comacho looked quickly at Mitch, as if surprised, then slowly placed his cup on the table as he stood to his full height, his eyes full of fire again, and pride.

"Because when I say priceless I mean as a means of educating our young people about our heritage. We are not Spain, we are a mix, a blend, a melting pot as surely as the United States is. I'm surprised at you, Mitch, you know what we are trying to do here," said Dr Comacho, looking at Mitch as he sat back down. Mitch started to mumble something about only wanting to help, but the Professor cut him off with a raised palm, "I'm sorry, amigo," he said quietly, shaking his head, "Maybe you're right, I guess I don't live enough in the real world. Yes, there are people who would pay well to own some of these things, but it would have to be illegal, black market. You see these things don't belong to me, to us, they belong to the government, and they have to be cataloged, filed and all that before they decide what to do with them."

"Well, I should have known there would be some red tape in there somewhere," Mitch said disconsolately, "But we can't give up, we have to keep working."

"That's right," shouted the Professor as he jumped up and slammed the table with the flat of his hand, "We'll not let a bunch of fat, stupid politicians stop us!" With that he went on another tirade, questioning the background and family tree of every official between there and the capitol. As the Professor got louder and wilder, the students and workers started shifting about, most obviously wanting to excuse themselves but not having the nerve to interrupt their leader. So when Mitch stood up and said it was time to get some rest, that they had work to do tomorrow, the group got up practically en masse and fled out, murmuring their good-nights and condolences, grateful to get out of the mess tent but confused about their future. They talked in low voices, almost in whispers as they walked through the camp, as if they were afraid that their voices would carry as clearly as the cold light of the rising moon across the immense, empty expanse of sky between the scruffy stubble of the jungle and the brilliant ceiling of stars above them as they gathered in little knots around the flaps of their tents. Dr Comacho sat quietly until nearly all were gone. "Mitch, come here, walk with me to my tent," he called after Mitch, "I know I'm drunk and obnoxious and I embarrassed a lot of good people tonight," he said as Mitch walked back to him. He put his arm around Mitch's shoulders as they headed for his tent at the end of the campground, "Do you know why I care some much about our heritage?" he asked, staggering back a half step and grabbing Mitch's arm to catch himself.

"Sure, it's your life's work, you should feel strongly about it," Mitch replied, steadying his friend by holding onto his forearm.

"No, no," the Professor said as tears came to his eyes and his voice choked, "It is for love, love of Elena's mother." He half- sobbed once and stood back from Mitch, standing very straight. "I'm sorry, Senor," he said formally, "I don't mean to burden you with my old personal problems." Mitch really didn't know what to say at this point, respecting the Professor's pride and his privacy, but it seemed obvious to him that the Professor needed to let something out, to face it. So he said non-committedly,

"Hey, love is a good reason for anything in my book." Dr Comacho turned at the flap of his tent and said,

"Ah, Mitch, you are a good man, my gringo amigo, I think you will understand." He turned and stared up at the billions of stars visible through the opening the campground made in the jungle canopy as a pensive, dream-like look came over his face, "I've seen you look at Elena," he said. He went on as Mitch just shifted his weight uncomfortably, "I'm sure you have noticed the high cheekbones, the dark eyes, that beautiful hair, well, she got all that from her mother." He paused again, looking down at the ground and kind if hugging himself by holding his elbows, "She was the most beautiful woman I have ever seen, but she was half Indian." He shook his head sadly as Mitch interrupted,

"From what you've said about the mix of cultures and from what I've seen, that shouldn't have been that big a deal."

"Well," said Dr Comacho, "We are going back a few years here, and I also come from an old, established, and well-to-do family. They sent me to the best schools to be educated and to learn proper behavior in society and they wanted me to marry someone of our class, not some half-indian girl from the provinces. Not that she was an uneducated hick, either, her father owned a big ranch and she was very correct in her manner and a friendly, outgoing person who genuinely liked people. But try as she might, she just was never fully accepted by the high society of the capitol or even our peer group at the University."

"Prejudice is really a very strange thing," Mitch reflected as the Professor paused, shaking his head sadly. Mitch flashed back to his own father's problems with the "Good ole' boys" of South Florida in the fifties, when after having moved the family down from New Jersey and working as a provisional member of the painter's union for over a year, and being well liked by everyone, bosses and workers alike, he kept getting "blackballed", or voted out, at the formal membership meeting to become a full member of the union. After the second vote, when he was still blackballed, his friend and sponsor Carl Underhill stood up and asked the membership why they suddenly didn't want "Charlie," which was the Americanized version of his polish name Casimir, in their union. Several confused "Good ole' boys" stood up and said of course they wanted Charlie, they just didn't want this "foreigner" (Mitch's father was born in Perth Amboy, New Jersey), Casimir Kowalski! "They weren't just prejudiced against black people in those days," remembered Mitch, "But Yankees, foreigners, women, Jews, just about anybody who wasn't a white, male Baptist." Mitch's father did eventually get into the union and was accepted for the person he was. He always preferred to make a joke out of the whole thing, saying, "A rose by any other name would smell as sweet, but obviously a Pollack by any other name smells sweeter!" "Hey, that's not very fair," muttered Mitch, coming back to the present, people can be really cruel, can't they?"

"Yes, they can," replied the Professor. He swallowed hard, then continued, "I'm not saying that it killed her, that she died of a broken heart, she was too strong for that, and she loved having Elena to take care of, but I knew her and I know it was one of the major disappointments of her life. So, after she died while Elena was still quite young, I set out to change these attitudes by the only methods I knew, my scholarship." Dr Comacho stood up straight as he wiped his eyes with the back of his sleeve, "I don't want Elena to face what her mother faced. So that's why I care so much, and why we have to keep going," he said wearily, breathing out a long sigh as he reached for the tent flap.

"Don't worry, Prof," Mitch said, "Elena loves you and you've got some good people behind you, too."

"Thanks, Mitch," the Professor said. "Well, goodnight now, I hope for sleep."

Chapter Six: Jungle Archeology

Of course the work did go on, day after sweltering day. If anything, conditions got even harder on the Professor's people. Equipment was getting worn, some of the tents were leaking when it was raining and smelling of mildew and rot when the sun was out. And of course the inevitable rice and beans just kept on coming, broken up occasionally by a monkey or capi bara stew and augmented by fresh local fruit. But the Professor's following of students, travelers and workers had turned into a pretty tough little group themselves. Teo never did get to like monkey meat, but he and Louis became fairly good at getting them. The graduate student's soft hands and sloped shoulders had become hard and strong and expert at wielding a machete, shovel, or hand pick. They had cleared the area around the main dig, what they hoped was a tomb, breaking up and clearing away many large rocks. They had chopped out roots of jungle plants as thick as a man's waist, and they had chopped down several tall, straight trees to rig a derrick over the main dig entrance. They had endured the blasting sun of the mid-day tropics and the slashing rain of jungle thunderstorms. They had learned to deal with chronic athletes foot, leeches, ticks, and mosquitoes. But these were dedicated people; many were just like Dr Comacho, only younger. And the results they were beginning to get justified both their excitement and their hard work. As they had gone deeper into the fissure that Louis had hidden in, the broken shards of pottery had become larger, more complete. At about twelve feet down it became apparent that the earthquake that had made the fissure and taken the shards to the surface had also shifted what appeared to be a large cap-stone or foundation block to the right a matter of some yards. Digging beneath the enormous stone and to the left had unearthed some intact, low-ceilinged chambers, which the Professor believed to be preliminary to the tomb of someone important, perhaps even royalty. Crawling along in the narrow passageways that they had unearthed so far gave Mitch that same eerie feeling that he had experienced on the steep staircase of the cleared pyramid. The Mayans were seemingly masters of placement and atmosphere, as evidenced by the fact that some of the large, main pyramids were built so that their north-south axis was aligned with true north, not magnetic north. How they were able to do this and why they did remains one of the many mysteries of Mayan history. Mitch thought about of the magnificent beach-side

ruin at Tulum that he had visited on an earlier
trip through the Yucatan. The main temple
there stands on the edge of a cliff overlooking a
Caribbean bay of blue-green water over a white
sand beach complete with palms and sea-
grape, commanding the most prominent and
advantageous spot for miles around. Mitch had
often thought that just the physical attributes
of the location would be enough to put even
the most callous person in a thoughtful mood.
All the major Mayan cities seem to have been
placed with similar care, although sometimes
with different results. Mitch remembered his
first trip down the gringo trail when he and
several other foolish young hippies from Florida
had hiked the seven or eight kilometers from
the modern town of Palenque to the site of the
ruins, scouring the intervening cattle pastures
for psychedelic mushrooms along the way.
Local ranch hands, complete with braided
lariats, leather chaps, and cowboy hats, looked
down disdainfully from their small horses at the
crazy gringos who were brewing up a
mushroom and orange pekoe tea on a little
camp stove that Mitch had brought along for

just that purpose. Not that the local people didn't know what the mushrooms were all about; the still influential shamans, or "brujos" having used them for a long time as powerful "allies" to help them achieve an out-of-body experience and to gain insight into the nature of reality, but they felt that the use of mushrooms was a serious, if not sacred, thing and that they should not be used recreationally, for cheap thrills, as they perceived the gringo hippies to be doing. Mitch had to admit that there was a lot of truth in their assessment of the situation because he himself had become interested in the mushrooms of Palenque when it seemed that every article he read about the Gringo Trail mentioned them. According to the trendy magazines of the day like High Times or Rolling Stone, for any true child of the sixties to go to Palenque and not do mushrooms would be like going to Bordeaux and not sampling the wine. But Mitch considered himself somewhere in the middle of the debate because he had first become interested in psychedelics as an aid to introspection through the writings of then popular sages such as Huxly and Leary. He had also read all the books that Carlos Casteneda had written about his experiences as an apprentice to a modern day brujo in America's Southwest. And while Mitch knew he didn't have the personal discipline to follow "the warrior's path to knowledge", as Casteneda put it, (it required total commitment over your whole lifetime), and although he had been known in the past to do a psychedelic at a party or a concert just for fun, he did hope to pick up some insight, some deeper reading of the fabric of life that had gone on here. "If I wanted cheap thrills I could have tripped at Disneyland," Mitch remembered thinking at the time. He needn't have worried though, for from the time they first arrived at the site of the ruins in a high valley surrounded by steep foothills that were the beginning of a great mountain range that continued as the backbone of a continent through the length of Southern Mexico, they were assailed by a dark, brooding presence, a presence of power, and death, and evil that threatened to overwhelm their heightened psyches. Maybe it was latent claustrophobia, but Mitch felt he could feel the suffocating horror of the slaves and concubines that had been buried with the ruler as he carefully negotiated the steep steps in the narrow passageway that led to the famous burial chamber at Palenque, in the very center of the largest pyramid. Mitch had endured the guide's spiel about the capstone of the royal tomb, which some interpret as an ancient Mayan controlling either a space vehicle or some kind of sophisticated telescope, and he had maintained his cool until they climbed the steps again and emerged at the top of the pyramid. There he joined several other suddenly respectful hippies sitting with their backs to the temple wall, staring out over the rest of the ruins for what seemed like a couple of minutes but actually turned out to be several hours, rousing themselves only when they noticed that the sun was almost gone, hurrying down to flee that valley on the last bus of the day.

"I guess it was as much the Mayans as the mushrooms," muttered Mitch to himself as he experienced the same oppressive feelings now as he entered one of the preliminary chambers of their find. These chambers contained several complete vases and bowls, which had probably held food offerings, and some simple weapons and basic tools, presumably for use in the afterlife. Even though these artifacts seemed pretty plain to Mitch and Louis, Teo and the grad students were all fired up about them. And they did have enough value to cause Dr Comacho to be away more than he wanted, setting up storage in the village where the finds could be held until transferred to a vault in Tovelado. This suited Mitch just fine because it meant spending more time with Elena. She and Mitch were practically running the dig now, Elena directing and cataloging, and Mitch taking charge of the work force. The only problem was that the building in the village was the warehouse of the pottery shop, which operated out of the back of the building, and also housed a small cantina where beer and wine were sold. Elena was a little worried that her father might start drinking too much again, what with spending so much time there and with the owner of the pottery shop, an old friend of the Professor's named Miguel. But she and Mitch had enough to think about now, as the hard work in the jungle and the clear, warm nights made for a hard, healthy, and satisfying existence for now. Some nights they would sit on top of one of the cleared mounds, with their backs to the dig beneath them, and stare out over the jungle, laid out like an ocean before them, the tops of the trees rippling away into the dark distance like breakers on a perpetually stormy sea. They would sit holding each other, watching as the moon rose and washed its white light over the endless jungle and the puny-looking efforts of man, both modern and ancient, the breeze blowing away most of the mosquitoes, and they would talk. One night, after they had sat in comfortable silence for a long while, Mitch ventured, "Elena, how do you feel about your mother?"

"What do you know about my mother?" Elena asked, sitting up and looking at Mitch suspiciously.

"I know she was very beautiful and your father loved her very much," Mitch replied softly. Elena relaxed and looked at Mitch with a certain sadness in her eyes,

"If you have been talking to father about her then you probably know as much as I do. He never talked to me about her much, maybe it was too hard for him, I don't know. But to me, she was a princess. You see, she died while I was very young, so if there was anything wrong in her life, I didn't know about it. To me she was perfect, a beautiful angel from heaven, and that's the way I'll always remember her." Elena sighed and sagged back into Mitch's arms, "I've always tried to live up to her image or at least act in a way that would earn her respect." Mitch looked down at her tenderly and said,

"I think you have succeeded admirably, and I'm sure she would be proud of both you and your father now." He turned and looked up at the multitude of stars seemingly smothering the earth all around, "I wish I could have known her too."

*   *   *

One particularly hot and gusty day, when any promise of moisture from the few black clouds that were driving the wind just raised the level of humidity and made the Professor's little band of workers and scholars feel even sweatier and more uncomfortable than usual, The Professor returned early from one of his frequent trips to Miguel's warehouse. It was not yet noon when he appeared on the edge of the pit that the tough little crew had excavated around the small chambers already unearthed in an effort to skirt them and find the main chamber. Mitch thought he looked even more tired than usual as he called down to Mitch, "Hey, amigo, how's it going?"

"Compared to what?" Mitch shot back, leaning on his shovel and smiling up at Dr Comacho, "No, really, it's going ok I guess, why?" The Professor squatted down on his heels and looked down at his scratched and dirty and sweaty but still loyal crew and asked,

"It's pretty hot to be working down there today, isn't it?"

"You're telling me," Mitch replied, wiping his forehead with a bandana, "But we are just about to break for lunch, anyway."

"Well, I think I can do better than that," Dr Comacho responded, standing up and turning to where Elena sat in the shade, "Elena, come over here for a moment, will you? What holidays are coming up?" Elena got up and walked over to her father's side, looked quizzically at him and then at Mitch and said,

"Well, there's All-Saints Day in a couple of weeks and I think . . ." The Professor interrupted her with a raised finger, saying,

"All- Saints Day, that's good enough," he turned back and pronounced over the pit,"I hereby declare this to be Early All-Saints Day . . . , take the rest of the day off!" "And by the way," he concluded with a smile, "I'm buying the cervesas in the mess tent!" The rest of the workers and students had stopped digging to listen to the Professor, but they hadn't put down their tools. Now they dropped their picks and shovels and buckets where they were and surged for the ladder, cheering and chattering and laughing. Mitch stood back and looked up to catch Elena's eye, but she just shrugged and smiled and started back for her tent. Mitch finally got his turn at the ladder and had just gotten out of the pit and headed for her tent when he was waylaid by Louis and Teo.

"Come on, pal," Teo said happily, putting his arms around Mitch's shoulders, "Let's go soak up some suds!"

"Yeah," Louis chimed in excitedly, "I hear Dr Comacho brought back several cases from Miguel's, come on, let's get some!" Mitch looked once towards Elena's tent, but then allowed himself to be propelled along by his friend's momentum toward the mess tent.

"Well, gee, I don't know," he said, winking at Teo, "Do you think that two or three cases will be enough for you, Louis?"

"Hey, I don't know either," Louis shot back, "Let's go find out!"

It really was a lively little gathering in the mess tent. To the local workers the opportunity for a free beer was more than enough excuse to party and the grad students, though maybe a little run down, were in good shape from their weeks of hard work and early nights and ready to party. Somebody brought out one of those ever-present portable tape players, known as "ghetto blasters" in the States and as "Salsa boxes" down south, and soon half the people were dancing, both inside and outside the mess tent, the saucy Latin disco music easily spilling out over the little clearing between the tents. Mitch sat back and sipped his beer as he watched the people party around him. Several of the couples among the students were boyfriend and girlfriend, though they were pretty low-key about it, and one couple of grad students was married. Mitch watched them now as they laughed and swayed and stamped their feet to the heavy rhythm and envied them. Here they were, starting out on their life's work together, young, happy, and pretty clear in the direction of their future. Mitch couldn't help but to contrast that to his own situation, that nagging feeling like a cancer at the back of his mind, that the days of his youth were slipping away, that the time of confusion and doubt that you can use as an excuse for not really doing anything with your life, that time when you were trying to find yourself before finding your future was coming to an end, and that he wouldn't be able to justify doing the things he liked anymore. "Yeah, and there's nothing sillier than someone trying to act like a teenager when they are pushing thirty," Mitch mused despondently to himself as he took another long pull on his beer. "Well, at least they have decent beer down here," he thought as he burped contentedly. Mitch considered himself something of a "beer snob", if there could be such a thing. He knew that "beer snob" was probably a contradiction in terms but he really felt that there was a marked difference between the many brands and that it was worth the price to get quality. First of all, he wouldn't touch any of the American commercial brands, considering them to be hastily cooked chemical elixirs designed to appease palates already conditioned by fast foods and frozen foods and a vast array of carbonated drinks to accept the lowest common denominator of taste. Secondly, he didn't like to drink anything out of a can, preferring instead glass bottles, especially the green ones, those usually denoting the strong but smooth German and Dutch lagers, Mitch's favorites. But, some of the Central American brews were quite good, Mitch finding Suprema and Bohemia to be pretty good, and of course the Dos Equis and Tres Equis consistently delivered quality. Mitch leaned conspiratorially over towards Teo and Louis sitting near the cooler. "Hey," he asked, "Why is drinking a "lite" beer like making love in a canoe?" Teo looked at him blankly and shrugged his shoulders, playing the straight man,

"I don't know. Why?"

"Because it's fucking close to water, that's why!" Mitch retorted, breaking himself up. The guys had just enough of a buzz on to think that that was really funny, and they were still laughing and snickering when they looked up to see Elena standing there.

"Hi, guys," she said gaily, "What's so funny?" Teo and Louis just kind of giggled and looked away like embarrassed schoolboys, Leaving Mitch to stammer out,

"Uh, you really had to be there," this causing another outburst of semi-squelched giggles from the guys. "But wait, wait," continued Mitch, recovering a bit of his rowdy attitude, "We weren't laughing at you, but judging from your outfit, we may have missed a good chance!" This caused Elena to put her fist on her jutting hip in exasperation and Teo and Louis and Mitch and several of the others who had heard the exchange to lose all control and explode into laughter, with Teo falling to one knee on the floor of the mess tent and Mitch pounding the table with one hand and wiping tears from his eyes with the other. It really wasn't all that funny but you would be surprised at what a couple of beers will do for you after a few weeks of jungle archeology. Elena's outfit did look a little out of place, though. She was standing on the dirt floor of the mess tent wearing sandals, a long, white beach dress, a floppy straw hat, large round black plastic sunglasses and holding a bottle of suntan lotion, a huge towel, and a small transistor radio. "Where are you going," asked Mitch when he had gotten hold of himself again, "Cozumel?"

"No, but I am going swimming," Elena replied haughtily, "I'm not going to waste this afternoon off just hanging around the mess tent drinking beer."

"Swimming? Where?" asked Louis
excitedly, jumping up and being echoed by
several, hot, sweaty, and interested people.

"Well, . . ., if you really want to know,
"Elena stretched it out, enjoying it now, teasing
them back a little and then giving in, "Okay,
Herman told me that there is a lake or pond or
something below a waterfall a little ways up
that creek that runs by here, and I'm going to
go up there and check it out. Anyone want to
come?"

"Wait a minute here, now," broke in
Mitch, waving his hand and shaking his head,
"A waterfall, a pond, this isn't any Mayan 'Well
of Souls' , is it?" He looked over at Teo and
shuddered, an exaggerated grimace on his face,
"I mean, the whole bottom isn't littered with
human bones, is it?"

"Oh, Mitch, quit fooling around,"
answered Elena with mock annoyance,
"According to Herman it's just a deep natural
pool in the little creek. He even said that he
would be kind enough to lead us there. Now,
whoever wants to go, go get your stuff together

and meet back here in five minutes, ok?"

"Ok, sure, sure," said Louis, jumping up
a little unsteadily and grabbing Mitch's arm,
"Come on you guys, let's go get ready!" He
turned back to Elena as they were headed out
the door, "Now, don't you leave without us,
okay?" he asked seriously.

"Yeah, don't let the tour bus leave
without us," Mitch put in, not quite so
seriously.

"Just get ready, "Elena replied, laughing,
"I'll be here waiting.

Mitch didn't know why, but he had to
admit he felt pretty excited as they got back to
their tent and started rummaging through their
backpacks for their bathing suits or shorts. He
didn't know if it was the beer, the jungle, or
Elena's coy smile as they were leaving the mess
tent, but his hands were shaking and there was
a burning sensation in the pit of his stomach as
he dug around in his pack for what he
considered the proper attire for the occasion.
First, his old standby cut-off jeans, which used
to be the most popular, if not only, choice of

gringo backpackers and young people everywhere, now slowly being replaced by the more fashionable khaki safari shorts or spandex yachting shorts, then his old flip-flop sandals, which he really didn't use much while traveling. It was generally too dirty in the cities and too buggy in the brush. He decided to top off his outfit with his Hawaiian-style flowered shirt, the one with the pictures of palm trees and little surfers on it. Throw in his knobby knees and his dark shades on a string around his neck, and Mitch was correctly dressed for any American beach party thrown between the early fifties and the present.

"You know what your trouble is, Mitch?" Elena asked when he and Teo and Louis had rejoined her at the mess tent.

"No, what, pray tell?" Mitch asked back, smiling.   "You've seen too many episodes of M.A.S.H., that's what," she replied, pointing her finger at him playfully.

"Yeah, I know it," Mitch responded, hanging his head, "It's called Hawkeye Pierce Syndrome, I can't help it, I just can't pass up the opportunity for a quip or a joke, no matter how good or how bad." He stepped over next to Elena and laid his head on her shoulder, his arms by his sides, "Can you help me, nurse?" he said, fluttering his eyelids up at Elena.

"I doubt it," she said, "Just try to restrain yourself, okay?" While this was going on they were joined by Herman and Perez and several of the grad students, the married couple among them, most carrying a folding chair or a towel and maybe a couple of beers to sustain them on their journey. Many of the students had opted to stay with the cooler and the salsa box, most of the local workers were already too drunk to go anywhere, and Dr Comacho had disappeared early to head back to Miguel's, so the little group was ready and set off down the jungle trail at the far side of the dig, laughing and singing with Herman in the lead. About five minutes into the brush, just when it seemed to Mitch that the trail was going to peter out altogether, it being almost entirely reclaimed by the jungle, the path intersected the bed of the little stream. They turned and started walking upstream, stepping from rock to rock along the banks as there wasn't any trail at all now. The water was clear and it was wonderfully cool and it felt good as they splashed themselves and each other as they hiked along. Not too far upstream they came to the place that Herman was talking about. Walking along the banks of the little stream, they had been in a sort of tunnel of vegetation, the foliage of the trees on either side growing up and out to join together over the creek bed, blocking out the sun almost entirely, so Mitch was blinking and reaching for his shades as they stepped into the bright sun of the clearing created by the pond below the waterfall. Mitch had to admit that after living and working these several weeks in the generally flat and densely overgrown jungle the waterfall and clearing were a pretty impressive, if unexpected, sight. The waterfall itself wasn't very large, but it was in the classic style, a narrow torrent of water about three feet wide flowing off a sharp edge and cascading about ninety feet down a sheer, steep cliff, widening out to around six feet in diameter before crashing into a pile of large boulders at the bottom of the precipice, creating a burbling, white wave of foam and a wonderfully cool mist. The festive group gathered in a little knot at the outlet of the pond into the creek, just standing there, looking around and taking it all in, almost mesmerized by the unexpected beauty of their surroundings. The few dark clouds scurrying across the sky couldn't block the sun out entirely or for long and the bright rays bouncing off the water droplets in the air made several small rainbows in the mist that spread out from the cascade and nourished the exquisitely colored wild orchids that hung in the trees surrounding their little Shangri-la, the encroachment of the trees stopped only by the round, smooth boulders of the riverbed. After several quiet moments Mitch turned to Herman and said,

"All right, Herman, this place is great! Thanks a lot for bringing us here." Mitch then turned to Teo as Herman smiled at the chorus of "Yeahs, okays, and graciases" coming at him from the rest of the gang, "So, Teo, what do you think? Is this a sinkhole we're in, or was this caused by the earthquake?" Teo looked thoughtfully at the sheer cliff wall,

"Probably an earthquake, like the one that moved our capstone." He was using his hands to illustrate his point, saying, "We must be right on the fault line here, and the one side rose as the other sank, and the river just kept on going, thereby . . .," when he was interrupted by Louis pushing by him.

"I don't care how it came to be, I'm just here to enjoy it," he said. With that he turned and jumped out into the pond, shirt, shoes, hat, sunglasses and all. He turned in the air to smile at them as he splashed down on his butt and sank entirely out of sight except for one hand holding up his beer, trying not to spill too much until he came up sputtering and gasping, standing on the bottom in the chest-deep water, with his straw hat sagging around his head and offered them a toast. What followed was the kind of hot summer afternoon at the old swimming hole that hopefully everyone has enjoyed at some time in their life. After all, a picnic is a picnic wherever it occurs. The finding a spot to spread out the blanket or towel, the tinny speaker of the transistor radio, the suntan lotion that makes you smell like a fruit salad, putting the beer in a little pool by the outlet of the pond to keep it cool, jumping off a rock to catch a Frisbee in the air before flopping into the water, maybe falling asleep in the sun and getting a little pink in areas that haven't seen a lot of sun lately. All of this was going on as the little party of workers and students relaxed and had a good time, enjoying their first real time off in weeks. Mitch was more than surprised, more like pleasantly shocked when he saw Elena's bathing suit. She had kicked off her sandals and pulled the beach dress over her head to reveal a black string bikini, like one you would expect to see on the beach at Rio de Janeiro, one of the kind that almost covered the front side of a woman but left very little to the imagination in back. In fact Mitch almost forgot to breathe as he stood in the water and watched her walk to the edge of the pond, his eyes flowing down from her black hair shining in the sun to her slender but smoothly muscled shoulders and arms flexing, the two tiny triangles of black cloth stretching over her small, firm breasts as she reached behind her to adjust the string holding the little top on. His eyes had slowly caressed their way down to the flat, smooth expanse between her navel and the top of her bikini bottom when he was rudely interrupted by Teo and Louis splashing water on him.

"Hey, buddy, "Teo said, grinning, "Put your eyeballs back in your head before they sink to the bottom and you lose them forever!"

"Yeah, and don't trip on your tongue getting out, either," put in Louis, laughing.

"Oh, yeah," retaliated a startled Mitch, "I'll show you guys who's boss." Then he jumped up on Teo, grabbing his head to try to dunk him, only to have Louis dive down and knock his legs out from under him, submerging them all in a thrashing knot of arms, legs, and heads, causing Mitch to miss Elena's graceful swan dive into the deeper part of the pond. Mitch didn't miss much else that Elena did that afternoon, though. He watched her rather awkwardly try to throw the Frisbee the way he was teaching her (All Florida beach boys being at least semi-expert at Frisbee), he watched her fold her arms to hold onto her bikini top as she stood laughing and sputtering under the natural shower of the waterfall. He saw her excitement as she led them behind the falling wall of water to show them a shallow cave she had discovered. And he saw her laughing and joking with the graduate students as they sat in the sun sharing beers, the women sociably brushing each others' hair between plunges into the cool water of the pond. As the afternoon wore on though, Mitch did begin to notice a subtle separation, a narrow gap between Elena and the workers and students, she being after all their boss, or the person who would grade their thesis someday. Several of the couples had already wandered off in search of the kind of privacy that is hard to find when you are living in a community of tents, and the rest, including Louis and Teo, were gathered behind a large rock and little ways downstream and on the opposite side of the pool from where Elena was sunning herself. Louis motioned for Mitch to join them as he disappeared behind the rock but Mitch preferred to swim over to talk to Elena. He pulled himself up on the rock next to her towel and let some of the cool water drip off his hand onto the small of her back. "Hey," she said, looking up and smiling, "How are you doing?"

"Oh, fine, fine," Mitch replied rather inanely as she sat up and turned to face him. "What's going on over there?" he asked, nodding in the direction the rest of the group had gone. Elena glanced over towards the rock and smiled, then turned back to Mitch with an amused look on her face.

"I'm surprised at you, you old hippie," she teased him, "You should know . . . it's Mota, you know, reefer, Marijuana?" Mitch was a little surprised himself, because he did smoke reefer, had for years and generally enjoyed it, but he was very careful about it when traveling, especially outside the U.S. He never tried to buy it while he was on the gringo trail but he would smoke it when it was available. He had been so into Elena that he hadn't noticed the subtle signals that everyone else had picked up that caused them to gather for the smoke.   "But why are they hiding it from you?" Mitch asked Elena, puzzled, "I mean, they were drinking beer and partying with you earlier."

"Oh," replied Elena nonchalantly, "It's just a courtesy, sort of. I mean, I know they smoke, they know I know they smoke, but it is still illegal and I am an assistant professor, so they don't embarrass me by sticking it in my face, see?"

"Right, I get it, that's pretty cool," said Mitch, "It means they have a lot of respect for you."

"Oh? And how about you," she asked, raising one eyebrow.

"Sure, sure," Mitch stammered, a little surprised, "I, ah, I respect you a lot . . ."

"No, no, no, silly, "Elena interrupted, laughing and waving her hand in front of her face, "Save that for later . . . I mean don't you want to go and get high?" Mitch's heart started pounding and his mind was going a mile a minute as he thought,

"Save that for later? Does that mean . . .? What does that mean?" but he just said, "No, that's okay, I'd rather just stay here with you." He reached down and took her hand from where she had let it fall in her lap and leaned in toward her face, hypnotized by her deep, dark eyes. Just then Louis came around the corner of the rock they were on.

"I hope I'm not interrupting anything," he said with a sly, conspiratorial grin, "I brought you two a present." He squatted down next to Mitch, put one hand on Mitch's shoulder and opened the other to reveal a couple of joints and a beat up pack of matches. "I didn't want you guys to feel left out, so I brought you these in case you wanted to toke up a little." He winked at Mitch as Elena smiled and Mitch said,

"Well, thanks, amigo, that's alright. Sit down guy," he continued as he took the joints and matches out of Louis's hand, "Let's fire one up right now."

"No, thanks," Louis replied, standing up and glancing at the dark clouds that were claiming more and more of the sky as the afternoon wore down, "I feel good already, and I also wanted to tell you two that most everybody else has decided to cruise on back to camp." He paused and looked down at them, their knees touching, their hands still close together on the towel from when they had reluctantly let go as Louis approached, their shoulders nearly touching as they subconsciously leaned in toward one another, and asked, "Do you want to come along with us now, or . . ." his voice trailed off as he looked questioningly at them, his arms spread out with his palms up. "It's up to you," he added as Mitch glanced quickly at Elena and then said,

"Well, no, I guess we'll stay here for a little while, smoke one of these doobies, then we'll be coming along behind you, okay?"

"Sure, sure, amigo, I understand," Louis replied, not quite successfully suppressing a smile, "You guys come along whenever you're ready, but," he continued, turning serious, "Don't wait too long, because there is probably less than a couple of hours of daylight left, and this jungle is no place to be lost in at night."

"Yeah, you're right," replied Mitch, thinking about what the mosquitoes would be like out there after dusk, "And I get lost pretty easy, too. Why don't you do me a favor and tie a towel or something on a tree where that trail meets the creek bed, okay?"

"Sure thing pal, no problem," Louis

answered, stepping to the edge of the rock, "Well, I'll catch you guys later, enjoy." With that he jumped out into the water in a long shallow dive that brought him back to the surface about halfway across the pond towards where Teo and the few partiers that were left had gathered for the hike back to camp. Mitch and Elena sat for several moments in awkward silence as the little band of pleasantly tired and definitely relaxed picnickers slowly zigged and zagged out of sight up the creekbed. Finally after the last of them had disappeared Mitch said,

"Well, I guess we might as well smoke one of these, ok?" He put the joint in his mouth and tore off a match to light it, then paused, took it back out and asked Elena, "You do smoke, don't you . . . I mean . . ." His confusion showed on his face as she cut in and said,

"Sure, I smoke, not a lot, but some, and why should that surprise you? I'm young, I'm in a university environment, so?"

"Well," Mitch replied, blushing a little as he let his eyes slide down and back up her body, "That's not the only thing about you that surprised me today."

"Oh, you like my bathing suit?" she
responded, smiling, "I could tell you noticed it."

"Oh, yeah, sure, it's a beauty," Mitch
stammered, really embarrassed now,
successfully resisting the urge to add, 'And so
are you', pretending to be absorbed in striking
the match and lighting the joint. Elena leaned
back and sat up straight as she reached out and
took the joint from Mitch as he sneezed a little
trying to hold in the smoke.

"Mitch," she said, giving him a hard
look, "Your provincialism is showing." She
paused to take a polite little drag on the doobie
as a surprised Mitch said "What?" as he blew
out a cloud of blue smoke, but she went on
before he could catch his breath, "Yeah, you
were surprised because all you North
Americans think anyone south of Los Angeles is
a hick, like we were all caught in a time warp or
something," she paused again to turn her head
to blow out her little puff and Mitch seized the
opportunity to protest, saying something about
not lumping everybody into one group, when
she interrupted him again by taking his hand in

both of hers and smiling, saying, "Don't worry, Mitch, I'm not upset, I'm just razzing you a little bit." She relaxed again, leaning against his shoulder, reminiscing now, "Besides, I guess it's true to a certain extent, I mean there is some resentment towards the U.S., but mostly it's a love-hate relationship." She laughed in a low throaty chuckle and looked up at Mitch's eyes as she said, "You should have seen me and my friends at the private, girls only prep school I went to in the capital. I mean we wore the same designer jeans popular up north, we danced to the same disco music that the Americans did, we tried to find some mota or a doctor to give us the pill, trying to be hip, like the North Americans, you know?"

"Yeah, I know what you mean," he replied, looking down at her and raising his eyebrows, "What's this about the pill?"

"Oh, Mitch," she answered, making a face of fake aggravation and sitting up again, "It was pretty funny, though." She smiled to herself, "There we were, all these spoiled little teenage girls in our school uniforms, going around trying to find a doctor to prescribe the pill, trying to keep our parents or anyone else except our close friends from finding out, and then looking at each other when we were finally successful and thinking, "Does this mean I have to go out and screw somebody?" She stopped and gave a little laugh, a wry smile on her face as she took the joint from Mitch, still remembering. But Mitch broke her pensive mood almost immediately by jokingly imploring her to go on, asking,

"Well, what happened after that? How old were you then?" But she interrupted him once again, standing up and saying flirtatiously,

"Oh, let's just say that I got over it all right." She smiled and handed him the considerably shortened joint. "Here, you handle this," she said, "I'm going to cool off again." She turned, took a step and plunged out into the cool, dark water, staying under for a considerable distance before popping up laughing and waving for him to come. He bent down to snub out the doobie on the rock, his hands shaking with excitement as he put the roach carefully behind the remaining matches in the matchbook and folded it up in his shirt.

He shook his head as he thought that even at a moment like this he was still too much of an old hippie to litter, even something little like a roach. "Funny how some of those hippie beliefs became ingrained," he mused as he stepped to the edge of the rock. He didn't feel like an old hippie just then, though. Judging from the knot in his throat, the butterflies in his stomach, and the sweat running down his back, he felt more like a nervous high-schooler on his first date. "Oh, well, here goes nothin'," he muttered as he took a deep breath and dove out towards the center of the pool and Elena. He came up near where Elena had been, wiped his hair back out of his eyes and looked around, but she wasn't anywhere to be seen. He turned to look back the other way when suddenly she burst out of the water behind him and grabbed him around the shoulders, pulling him off balance as she tried to drag him under. Mitch struggled to get his feet back under him and reached behind and got her around the waist, pulling her over in front of him, both of them laughing as their arms wrestled around under the water, Mitch more and more in control as she came in front of him. Gradually the horseplay slowed as Elena's struggles got weaker and more half-hearted as their faces got closer and he drew her up toward him, her struggles finally stopping altogether as they stared for a long moment into each other's eyes, then kissed as he bent towards her and she rose ever so slightly to meet his lips. It began as a tentative, wondering kiss, one that had been thought about for weeks, as they held each other in the waist deep water and gently and slowly let their lips explore each other's feelings, then it evolved into a passionate, physical intermingling of desires, showing with the firm, purposeful pressure of thighs and chests and the almost urgent interplay of tongues the inevitable direction of their passion. Suddenly Elena broke away from him and swam towards the waterfall, laughing and looking back over her shoulder. Mitch just stood there feeling light- headed, breathing deeply and feeling the rush of blood around his body as his heart pounded away in his heaving chest, watching Elena as she reached the pile of boulders and started climbing towards the splashing cascade. Mitch was still standing there as she stood in the falling torrent with the water pouring over her taut young body, her beautiful long hair flowing in waves down to the small of her back. Then, whether she had untied it or just not tried very hard to keep it on, her tiny bikini top washed off, with Elena laughing as she bent forward to grab it before it was carried away by the flow, then slowly and deliberately standing straight up at the edge of the rushing column of water, looking at Mitch with a sultry, questioning look, throwing her head back as the water hit her shoulders and flowed over her firm, flawless breasts, her dark brown nipples hard from the cool caress of the falling water. She dove in and swam slowly back to the rocks their towels were on, with Mitch watching her perfectly rounded bottom, her upper thighs tight from their hard work and simple diet flashing in the foamy flow of her deliberate strokes. Mitch paused for the briefest of moments, wondering what he was getting into, but he knew if he didn't swim over there right then, he would regret it for the rest of his life.

Besides, he knew that it was over anyway, what with his heart, his brain, and every cell of his body rushing with excitement and desire. He surged forward, swimming with powerful strokes toward the rocks where Elena waited. He noticed right away that she hadn't put her top back on, the less than a handful of cloth lying crumpled and tangled by her side as she smiled at Mitch and patted the towel next to her. He made his way over to her and stretched out beside her, gently putting his left hand behind her head and his right across her waist to softly rub the curve of her back as he drew her face in to kiss her, the last of her small smile melting away just before their lips met. They kissed passionately for several minutes, Elena sighing, "Oh, Mitch," as she gasped in quick, shallow breaths as his mouth tasted the delicate softness of her neck and nibbled the tiny masterpiece of her earlobe. Mitch drew back and looked into her deep brown questioning eyes, and said, "I . . .," but she stopped him with a finger to his lips, "Don't say anything, Mitch, just let it be." Mitch smiled gratefully, warming with incredible passion for

the beautiful woman that he held so close.
Suddenly he noticed a jungle flower, a beautiful
orchid on the bush behind her. He reached out
and plucked it, a large, open orchid, mostly
colored a pure, rich white, but with each
delicate petal edged in purple, beginning in a
deep, dark purple at the base, and softening to
a pale lavender at the tips. He smiled as he
presented her his gift, saying, "The most
beautiful flower in the jungle for the most
beautiful woman in the world." Elena reached
out and gently took it from him, placing it
carefully behind her ear, his eyes involuntarily
dropping from the flower to the rising of her
beautiful bare breasts as she put her arms
around his neck, as she murmured, "Oh, Mitch,
you are such a gentleman," and then she kissed
him and drew him down on top of her as she
lay back on the towel, the last long rays of the
afternoon sun warming them as they made
love in the open air, as natural as the millions
and billions of God's creatures that lived and
loved in the teeming and profligate jungle
surrounding them.

Chapter Seven: Rick Archetti

Mitch didn't know when the feeling of unease, of suspicion, had begun to creep into his head or what had caused it. It couldn't be the dig, because things were going great and had been since the money started coming in. Dr Comacho had finally found a source of money, and the new equipment and supplies were making life, and work, easier. Also the dig was living up to it's promise as a treasure trove of near perfect artifacts. When the royal tomb was found and opened it contained a complete human skeleton and a complete set of burial relics, including slaves and concubines buried with the king. But the main find and crowning achievement was the ceremonial jade mask and necklace the skeleton was wearing, which was even more spectacular than the one they had seen in the museum. To the Professor and his students this meant proof of a royal tomb and that theirs was a major find in their field, and proof that all their hard work hadn't been for nothing. Maybe it was when the Professor had immediately rushed their finds off to the warehouse in the village that Mitch's nagging paranoia had started, and maybe it wasn't Dr Comacho's actions but his attitude. Maybe it was the man himself, the way he still looked harried and under pressure when he should have been reveling in his triumph. Maybe it was the way he kept drinking, spending time away from the dig where Mitch knew he wanted to be. Maybe it was the way he looked after each trip to Miami, where he had to go to meet with the group of private investors who were now financing the dig almost entirely. Elena was still worried about him, but didn't feel uneasy the way Mitch did; she knew her father was under pressure but put it down to the normal stress of handling a major dig. Besides, she was caught up in the high spirits now, too. Mitch could see she really enjoyed her work, flushed with pride and excitement and genuine fervor about her father's cause. Watching her crawl into the narrow passageway that they had dug under the capstone, pushing her hair back and wiping the sweat off her forehead as she sat on her scruffed old sneakers and laboriously sketched the position of every artifact in the tomb, Mitch could almost see the satisfaction radiating from her. "And why not?" Mitch thought. Things were going good, her father had been vindicated, the find was an important one that could really boost her career, and she was up to her elbows in something she really enjoyed doing. And Mitch had had to content himself with mostly watching her because ever since the money started coming in and the dig really got going it seemed as if their relationship had been put on hold. Besides the normal constraints of life in such a small tent village and Elena's position as second in command of the project, as well as both of their busy schedules, it almost seemed as if they had an unspoken understanding to let it ride for a while, to not push it for now. While it was obvious that the physical attraction hadn't changed, maybe even gotten stronger, Mitch was somewhat relieved to find that Elena,instead of seeing their romantic interlude at the waterfall as evidence of commitment, chose to see it as a confirmation of the potential of their relationship, whichever way it might go in the future. For now, it felt good just to know it was there. Mitch brought his thoughts back to the Professor and his worries about him, contrasting Elena's happy excitement with his pretty much unfounded uneasiness."Maybe I did too much scamming in my younger days," thought Mitch,"I guess I'll always be a little paranoid."

Mitch's paranoia wasn't helped any by

the arrival in camp of one Richard"Dick"
Archetti, personal representative of one of the
private investors. Young, good-looking, and
flashy, he was one of those guys you wanted to
dislike but couldn't find a reason to. He dressed
well in a style that would have been low-key
and smooth in Miami, but did stick out a little in
the jungle. From his Vuarnet shades hung from
a string around his neck, past his Sportif shorts
and Rolex watch, down to his slightly scruffed
Top-siders, he was correct, clean, and pressed.
He was straight forward without being
aggressive, he looked you in the eye when he
talked to you and he remembered your name.
Still, Mitch didn't like the way he was always
hanging around, talking to Elena about the
inventory, bullshitting with Teo and Louis about
the work (he appeared to know construction
somewhat, said he had been with the union),
riding with Dr Comacho down the road his
bosses' money had improved between the dig
and the village and the village and the airport.
Mitch particularly didn't like Acrhetti's attitude
toward Elena, with him coming on to her like
the campsite was just a big outdoor version of

the flashy discotheques and singles bars he
frequented in Miami, pulling back her chair in
the mess tent, smiling and winking at her all the
time, and even asking her to go to his hotel bar
with him for a drink. His kind were all over
South Florida, Mitch having seen them in the
beach front restaurants of Fort Lauderdale,
driving fancy sports cars and drinking expensive
wines, spending hundreds of dollars on lunch as
they flashed wads of cash, proud of their
expensive lifestyle. Trouble was, most of the
money was bad money, coke money gathered
over the ruined lives of thousands of working-
class slobs and abused street people. "Plus,"
thought Mitch cynically," if you hung around
long enough you could see that these guys just
come and go, 'Top of the world, Ma' one
month, and history the next." And although
there were women who did seem to be
impressed by these self-styled movers and
shakers, Mitch could see that Elena wasn't
going for any of it from Mr Rick Archetti. Still, it
irritated him and probably bruised his male ego
that Archetti would dismiss him so easily as a
rival, just kind of laughing off anything between

Mitch and Elena and making his plays for her right in front of Mitch. One night Mitch was sitting in his tent with Teo and Louis, grousing about everything in general and Mr Archetti in particular. "What a slick," grumbled Mitch, "What's his interest in all this? Why has he got to see everything?"

"Well, I guess that's his job," Louis said with a sly smile, "I wonder if it is his job to pay such close attention to Elena, too?"

"That has nothing to do with it," Mitch shot back, "Besides, anyone can see he just sized up the local talent and decided Elena was the only blue-chipper around, and Elena is too smart for that."

"Ok, what is it then," demanded Teo, holding back a chuckle, "Are you jealous of the time he spends with Dr Comacho ,too?"

"No, I just wonder," replied Mitch, "Think about it. What are the private investors getting out of this?"

"They are affiliated with a major museum, and they get the satisfaction of bringing these artifacts to the world," answered Teo.

"Spoken like a true scholar, Teo, but do you really buy that? Do you, Louis?" demanded Mitch, "Besides, which museum; why hasn't it been named, publicized? I just don't think that people that would hire Dick Archetti would do anything for nothing, I just don't like it." Mitch sat down, finished.

"Well, what are we going to do about it, then?" asked Louis.

"I don't know, exactly," mused Mitch, "But I'd like to get a look inside that warehouse."

"You mean spy on Dr Comacho, follow him and watch him?" asked Teo with a shocked look.

"Yes, but it is for the good of the project," replied Mitch rather lamely, "I just want to see what these people are up to."

"Sort of 'All's fair in love and war', eh, amigo?" smiled Louis.

"Look at it any way you want, "Implored Mitch," are you with me?"

"Sure, sure, I'll go, just kidding around," replied Louis, "What about you, Teo?"

"I'll go, but under formal protest," said

Teo seriously.   "Protest noted," laughed Louis, "But what about Elena? Should we include her in?"

"No, don't tell her anything," Mitch said earnestly, "She's got enough to worry about already."

"What time do we pull this caper then, amigo?" asked Louis, "At midnight, or do we wait for a full moon?"

"A thousand miles out in the goddamned jungle and I'm surrounded by comedians," Mitch said with a smile, "Just meet me in the old campground around four o'clock. I'll tell Elena we're going fishing or something."

So the three conspirators met in the old camp, where they waited in one of the back chickees for the Professor to come by in his jeep. They talked about hiding in the back of the pick-up truck that was taking the latest accumulation of artifacts into town, but they couldn't figure out how to avoid detection once they arrived at the warehouse. So they resolved to walk the several kilometers into town, reluctantly on Teo's part, but Mitch used his rough Spanish and considerable charm to borrow a couple of old bicycles. They were looking them over, trying to tighten a few things when the Professor sped by, with Archetti in the jeep and the pick-up close behind. "Ok guys, this is it," said Mitch excitedly as he pushed the bike onto the road, "Let's go!" This was great," he thought, "I've actually got a little of the old adrenalin going again."

"Hey, what, you get a bike all to yourself while we have to tow?" asked Louis with mock bitterness, "Who died and left you the leader?"

"Louis, will you stop razzing me, this is serious." Even as he said it Mitch couldn't help smiling. And even though his adrenalin rush soon wore off in the late afternoon heat, Mitch still felt pretty good. Maybe he felt a little guilty about spying on Elena's father and maybe a little confused about his own motives, but it was great to be out on this recently reworked coral rock road, on an adventure with a couple of good partners, this was living to Mitch. They pumped steadily along on the old bikes for a while, the chains creaking and the loose and bent fenders rattling with every bump, when suddenly Teo's bike popped a tire, sending him and Louis sprawling in an almost comical spill onto the narrow shoulder. "Damn," said Mitch after he had made sure they were all right, "I guess we'll have to walk the rest of the way."

"Ok, but what about the bicycle?" asked Louis. "Bring it along, we can probably get it fixed in the village while we do our thing," replied Mitch.

"Whatever our thing is, "Teo muttered dispiritedly as they walked the last bit into town. They came into town on the main road but turned off at the first side street. Usually the sight of two tall gringos and a short one pushing two old, beat up bicycles down the dusty side street would not go unnoticed in such a small town, and it didn't this time either, but the Professor's project had been going on long enough now for the locals to be used to seeing his people around. As the adventuresome trio made their way along the street, checking out the shops on either side trying to find a place to get the flat tire fixed, Mitch reflected again on some of the small pleasures of life on the gringo trail. The delicious aromas from the local bakery, or panteria, spilling out onto the sidewalk, commandeering their noses as they reluctantly passed by, the bright colors of the women's dresses and the unfinished designs on the fabrics in their looms, contrasting with the faded pastel shades of the building as they sat in the doorways or just in the street out front, weaving with amazing speed as they laughed and talked amongst themselves, the friendly smiles of the firemen in the driveway of the firehouse, washing and polishing a Dodge fire truck that had to be at least forty years old. Impressions like these and countless others coming at you in a constant stream were what made Mitch feel so alive on the trail, what made him enjoy traveling so much...that and the feeling of freedom, and of being somebody a little different, special somehow. He knew you actually are special while traveling, representing a strange and alien culture in just about every place you went. As long as you didn't hang around long enough to become ordinary, that is. Mitch was brought out of his reverie by Teo pointing down the street and saying,   "There, on the corner, isn't that a garage?"

"Yeah, that's it," replied Louis as he started across the street wheeling the heavy, sluggish old cruiser ahead of him, "Let's get rid of this thing and get on with it." Mitch looked ahead to see an old man wiping his hands on a rag as he stood in the shade of the open garage door in a low, ugly concrete block building, painted a dark green with a few signs and company logos fading away above the door. The cool, dark interior of the garage felt great after the heat of the street and Mitch stood blinking his eyes in the shadows just inside the door, close enough to outside to still be in the breeze as Louis showed the old man the flat tire. As his eyes adjusted Mitch looked around the small town garage, with a rack of tires against the wall, a few old fan belts hanging from the ceiling, a shelf with a few cans of oil and some boxes of spark plugs on a table in the back, a few tools hanging from a pegboard on the wall, and of course a couple of old men taking their ease lounging against the side wall, watching all the goings on. There was also an old dog lying in the shade just inside the door, taking advantage of the breeze just like Mitch was, and a little ratpack of kids, boys mostly, hanging around. They gathered around the guys, laughing at their bikes and asking questions about what it was like living out in the jungle on the dig, or just marveling at Teo's height. The guys left the bikes with the old mechanic, who promised to fix the flat and also give them a badly needed lube job. Then they continued up the side street until they were about a half a block from the warehouse. "Hey, wait a minute," said Teo, "Do you think we ought to go through with this, in broad daylight and all?"

"Come on, man, it's nearly evening now anyway," said Mitch encouragingly, "All the locals are in their casas having dinner. Nobody cares anyway. Just act like you know what you're doing." With that Mitch started down the street toward the back of the warehouse. After hesitating a few moments, and then starting, stopping, and starting again, Teo and Louis fell in behind. They had almost caught up with Mitch when they were surprised to see him, after stopping by the door for a quick glance up and down the street, reach back, open the door and step into the warehouse. They didn't know what to do and just stood there alternately staring at the door and glancing furtively around the street until they saw Mitch's arm appear at the door, waving them on. They hurried to the door and stepped in, seeing only a quick glimpse of Mitch's face with a finger to his lips before the darkness of the old building engulfed them. After their eyes adjusted a little they could see that there was some light in the warehouse, coming from an office near the front. The guys huddled down next to Mitch behind some large crates in the back corner of the building.

"Is this our stuff?" whispered Louis to Mitch, indicating the crates they were hiding behind.

"No," answered Mitch, shaking his head, "Pottery supplies, for Miguel, probably. Those are ours over there, I think," he went on, pointing to several smaller crates stacked near the office.

"Let's have a closer look at them, then," said Louis.   "No," replied Mitch, "There's somebody in the office over there, let's wait until they leave. . . . oh, shit, they're coming in here!" Teo, Louis, and Mitch scrunched down as small as they could behind the crates as the light from the office flooded the room and three men stepped into the warehouse and up to the dig's crates. One was Miguel, the owner of the warehouse and pottery shop, the others were Dr Comacho and Rick Archetti. Even though this was Miguel's place, it was obvious by his attitude and body language that he was not in charge of whatever was going on now. When they reached the segregated group of boxes and crates, both large and small, Miguel hung back, leaning against a crate behind Dr Comacho, not saying a word, the nonchalant, even bored look on his face betrayed only by a cold glitter in his hard, black, Indian eyes as he watched Rick and listened to the Professor's and Rick's conversation. Even though both the Professor and Archetti were addressing themselves to each other and pretty much ignoring Miguel, Mitch could see that the Professor didn't do it with the same studied arrogance that Archetti did. "What a son-of-a-bitch," Mitch thought angrily, "Whenever he is in a position of superiority he really likes to grind it in." There was no clue to Miguel's feelings on his dark, impassive face but Mitch knew that his fierce Mayan blood had to be boiling. Mitch knew from talking to Elena when they were worried about Dr Comacho drinking too much that he and Miguel went back a long way. When Dr Comacho had first arrived in this area many years ago, a naïve young professor from a proper and respected family of the capital, Miguel was the one local to take him in, to guide him, to get him the connections in the local community and to help him gain the valuable experience he needed to launch his long and successful career. Now that they were still friends after all these years they had become known as something of the local odd couple, the short, heavy-set shopkeeper and pottery maker from the village and the tall, patrician scholar from the big city. Mitch thought the addition of the young urban slick from the U.S. really made for a strange trio indeed as he strained to hear what they were saying.

"You see, Rick," Dr Comacho was saying as they came in, "Everything is ready for you, all crated up and ready to go." He picked up one of the smaller boxes, "See, sturdy cardboard around lightweight foam."

"Yeah, well, how do I know what is in it if it's already boxed?" asked Archetti a little suspiously, "I'm responsible to some heavy people, you know."

"Rick, you don't trust us by now?" smiled the Professor, holding his arms out palms up in front of him, the small box still in his hand.

"Sure I do, Doc," Archetti replied, smiling thinly, "I trust you guys ok but these aren't school administrators or local officials we're dealing with here. These are rich and powerful men, men who are used to getting what they want, no matter what it takes."

"Well, they can't expect too much, you know, because most of what we are finding is too important in terms of research and national heritage to let out of the country," Dr Comacho retorted, a little exasperated, "Besides, when I met them, they all seemed like knowledgeable and reasonable men, surely they will understand?" Archetti sighed deeply and patiently, as if he were trying to explain something to a backward child, and said,

"Sure, they're sophisticated and friendly socially, they can afford to be, but when it comes to collecting they can get pretty serious . . . it's like a big game to them, an ego game with each one wanting to have a better collection than the other, and they will go to great lengths to get it." He glanced over at Miguel eyeing him impassively and then back at Dr Comacho, who didn't say anything but was rubbing his chin with a worried frown wrinkling his face, "Surely you heard about that museum in Mexico City . . .?" Mitch stiffened and he and Teo and Louis looked at each other incredulously as the Professor replied, highly agitated,

"Mexico City! Why that was an outright robbery! Surely you're not telling us that you had anything to do with that? And those men I met, no, I don't believe that!"

"Whoa, calm down now, Professor," Rick answered, stepping back and spreading his arms out in a calming gesture, a smug smile on his lips, "It's not polite to ask someone a question like that, you know. And I was just trying to illustrate the lengths to which some of these collectors will go to get the pieces they want. Of course I'm not talking about any of the people that we are working with, ok? Come on Doc, it's gonna be cool, don't worry. Let's get back to the problem at hand, how 'bout it? "Rick said, smooth and friendly again. Dr Comacho still seemed a little dubious, looking worried and unconvinced, but he turned to Miguel, handed him the box he was holding and said,

"Here, Miguel, open this for Rick."

"Not that one," broke in Rick, pointing to a larger one on the floor, "That one, the big one there."

"Ok, Miguel," said the Professor, "Go ahead, open it." Through this conversation Mitch, Louis, and especially Teo had been frozen still, trying to be as quiet as possible.

They slowly relaxed a little as they regarded the stark contrast between the edges of light and shadow in the irregularly stacked warehouse. They were definitely in the shadow, being both in the corner and behind some large crates. So, while the three men were busy opening the packing crate, Teo raised his head a little to see what was inside it. When he came back down he was all agitated, his eyes bugging out of his head and his Adam's apple bobbing up and down as he gulped furiously. Mitch held his hands up to calm him and cautioned him to be quiet. He settled down but Louis and Mitch could see he was dying to tell them something. But Mitch put a finger to his lips and then to his ear, nodding his head towards Rick and Dr Comacho and Miguel. Teo got the idea and they all strained to listen. "So, are you happy now, Rick?" said Dr Comacho with his hand on Archetti's shoulder, "Those pieces are ready to be shipped out, and we have a couple of small pieces for you to take back personally."

"Ok, but how is that going to work?" asked Rick, apparently satisfied with the crates.

"Oh, Miguel here is a great artist with

pottery and he has covered them with local clay, so that they resemble the souvenirs of the ruins that the locals sell to the tourists every day here. You won't have any trouble going out," replied Dr Comacho as the three men walked back into the office and shut the door. Plunged back into darkness, Mitch, Teo, and Louis just sat there in silent shock for a long time, in fact until they heard the Professor's jeep start up and drive away. Then they all got up and hurried out, walking quickly down the street, looking around at the corners and hugging the buildings all along. Nobody said anything until after they had retrieved the bicycles from the garage, paid the mechanic, and were on their way back up the road to camp.

Finally Teo couldn't contain himself anymore and said excitedly, "That's our stuff in those boxes," he practically shouted, "One of the most perfect friezes we've found!"

"Calm down, Teo, you're going to crash again," said Louis from the handlebar of Mitch's bike, where he was because he didn't want to ride with Teo again. "But what about it, Mitch," he asked, "That stuff isn't supposed to leave the country, is it?"   "What do you mean, 'what about it'," snorted Mitch with an 'I told you so look', "It's pretty obvious where the money has been coming from; the Professor has sold out. He must be selling the stuff to 'private investors' in Miami."

"That can't be true," broke in Teo angrily, "The Professor is a man of honor, he wouldn't do that."

"Yeah, you're right, Teo," Mitch replied sadly, "It just doesn't figure with him. But then how do you explain what we saw and heard?"

"Yeah, and how do you explain it to Elena," mused Louis, "This could really hurt her."

"Don't say anything to Elena, then," begged Mitch, "Not for now, not until we talk to Dr Comacho about this, okay?"

"Sure, it will be our secret for a while," agreed Louis as Teo nodded his assent.

Chapter Eight: The Ants

The next few days at the dig were really strained. The guys couldn't confront Dr Comacho because he had gone to Miami again with Rick, with Mitch saying that it was because Rick had gotten paranoid about the small objects he was supposed to take out and made the Professor come along. Louis and Teo just nodded their heads glumly when they heard this but Teo for one was beginning to have his doubts. He felt the Professor should be given a chance to explain and until he had that chance they shouldn't condemn him. Mitch and Louis agreed and tried to throw themselves into their work with their old enthusiasm but it was very difficult to do. Mitch was really worried about Elena, about how she would take it if she knew, whether they should tell her, or how to shield her from the truth if they wanted to. Herman and Perez could tell something was different between the guys but because they could see that none of the guys wanted to talk about it they didn't press. Mitch was grateful for that and confined his conversations with them to the logistics of the dig. In the late afternoon of the third day of the Professor's trip, Mitch was getting an inventory of tools needed from Herman and Perez when Elena approached and said, "Can I talk to you for a minute, please, Mitch?" Mitch said 'Sure' but got a sinking feeling in the pit of his stomach when he saw Herman and Perez backing away looking at the ground, excusing themselves profusely, and then turning around and walking away talking quietly between themselves.

"Oh, shit,"thought Mitch,"what does she know?"

"Mitch," Elena began, "I've been getting strange feelings around here lately, is there something going on that I don't know about?"

"Strange feelings?" Mitch replied innocently, "What do you mean? Maybe everybody is just tired."

"Tired?" Elena said with an edge in her voice as she looked sideways at Mitch, "Not too tired to ride a bicycle into town, not too tired to follow my father and Rick. What did you hope to find out?"

"Now, wait a minute, Elena," Mitch replied soothingly, "What are you talking about?"

"Oh, come off it, Mitch," cried Elena, her voice rising and tears coming to her eyes, all the strain and exhaustion of the past months on her face as she stepped closer to Mitch and said quietly, "Herman told me you guys had a flat tire fixed in the village the day you said you were going fishing, and when I asked Teo about it he turned all tongue-tied and practically ran away, so, I know something is up. No more lies please, just tell me what is going on." During this conversation Teo and Louis were walking back to camp after working all day on the other side of the dig. But when they saw Mitch and Elena standing together in heavy conversation they stopped. They didn't want to walk by and be drawn into it, so they just milled around, Teo pretending to show Louis some hieroglyphs nearby. Mitch looked imploringly at Elena and said,   "Elena, please don't embarrass us with your questions, we just went into town to have some fun." With that he looked toward Teo and Louis for some moral support, but they would have none of it, just shuffling their feet and looking down, avoiding Mitch's glance. Elena looked up at Mitch and stepped so close that his arms went around her almost as a automatic reflex. With tears in her eyes she said,

"Come on, Mitch, I know you guys and I know that there is no 'fun' to be had in the village, so tell me the truth, I am part of this group and I have a right to know." Mitch glanced again at Teo and Louis but again they looked away so he made his decision.

"Listen," he said to Elena, "You really want to know, even if it hurts?"

"Yes," she said quietly.

"Well, I'll tell you what we know now, without making any conclusions, and remember we don't know the whole story yet, okay? 'Mitch admonished her gently. He then told her the entire tale of their adventure, the warehouse, the conversation between Rick and her father, the crates, all of it. The whole time he was talking Elena just clung to his arms, becoming more and more confused and angry as her mind was torn between listening to and denying what Mitch was saying or looking at and examining her own doubts and anxieties about her father that had forced themselves into her thoughts, her eyes seeming to glaze over as she sank farther and farther into herself. Even after listening to Mitch and trying to assimilate the disturbing idea of Mitch sneaking around and spying on her father, she was recalling her own private worries about her father, about his travels to Miami, about how much time the business side of their profession took away from his time on the dig, where she knew he would much rather be. And although she respected her father and his position, and because she herself was involved in the life of a professional scholar, she knew how much determination and hard work it had taken him to build and maintain the reputation he now enjoyed, she still wondered whether he was in over his head in such a large, sophisticated, international center like Miami. She knew he was much more the idealist than the pragmatist but she thought that he had been especially vague when she had asked what museum was ultimately supposed to get the pieces and when they were going to send over some members of their staff to inspect the dig. He had said something about a deal being in the works that would be finalized later, and also that the investors that he had met were all decent men with good standing in the community, that it was all on the up and up. He had tried to reassure her, and she had told him that it was all right, but it had still left her wondering, because she didn't think that she had implied that it wasn't on the up and up.

"Something's just not right about this deal," she thought, "And what about this Rick Archetti, where does he fit in?" The guy didn't act like any other museum representative that she had worked with, and although he came on real smooth and friendly there was just something about him that made her nervous. Even when he was trying to flirt with her she could tell that he did it more to irritate Mitch than with any real interest. She wondered if her father knew about his associate's streak of meanness or if he even wanted to see it. And she had to admit that Archetti's money had certainly made life easier on the dig and had speeded up their progress considerably. In spite of her inner turmoil she remained calm, and when Mitch had finished she looked at him dully and asked, "Well, what do you make of it?"

"Oh, come on, Elena," Mitch said softly, gently shaking her by the shoulders, "Those crates were marked for Miami, not Tovelado,, and where do you think the money . . ." At this point all the pent-up frustration and denial in Elena broke through as she twisted out of Mitch's arms and started slapping him, crying and screaming,

"You lie, you liar, my father would never . . ., you're a pig, a gringo pig, get out of my sight!" Her hands trembled and tears ran down her red, flushed cheeks, flying off her chin as she shook her head from side to side, gulping and sobbing as she tried to continue yelling at Mitch, but nothing would come out, so she turned away and gripped her arms across her chest, hugging herself and sobbing violently. A confused and hurt Mitch just stood there helplessly for a few seconds, softly repeating her name over and over, hoping to calm her down.

Teo and Louis got over their initial reluctance and started to approach slowly, surprised at her outburst and worried, wanting to reassure her, but not exactly sure how. Mitch stepped over next to her again and reached out sympathetically to put his hands on her shoulders when she punched him in the chest with both hands and screamed, "No, No, No, you pig, get away from me!" Suddenly she turned and ran blindly across the dig and into the jungle. Mitch, Teo, and Louis just stood there stunned for an instant and then started after her. Mitch had the lead and as he crashed into the darkening gloom of the jungle he stopped and yelled, "Hold it guys, it'll be dark soon, I'll go after her, you guys go back for lights and help, okay?"

"Okay," shouted Louis as he and Teo

backed out of the thick brush, "Stay with her, brother, we'll be back right away!"

With that Mitch turned and plunged full bore into the jungle, crashing through wet leaves, ripping past vines tangling his arms and ankles, falling hard a couple of times, scraping up his arms and hands pretty good. He hadn't gone fifty feet when he realized that he couldn't hear Elena moving anymore and he was losing track of directions himself. He stopped and stood stock-still and strained to listen in the strangely quiet rain forest. Their ruckus had put down the birds and monkeys that usually make all the noise, but it hadn't daunted the insects, many of which started to find Mitch frozen there. Mosquitoes buzzed around his head, while gnats gnawed on the back of his neck and wrists, with various other itches all over his body from brushing by bugs or stinging plants while running or falling. He stood there in near silence and then broke it by calling her name. "Elena, Elena," his voice rang through the evening darkness under the jungle canopy. In the contrasting quiet when he stopped he heard her sobbing. The canopy of branches above them played tricks with the sound and Mitch couldn't tell if she was five feet or fifty feet away. "Elena," he begged, "Stay still and let me find you, I will get you back to camp, Teo and Louis and Herman and Perez will be coming real soon to help us."

"No," she screamed, "Stay away from me, everybody stay away from me!" Mitch could hear her jump up and start running again, crashing through the leaves and branches, sounding just like a Tapir or a large Capi Bara like the ones they had hunted around here. But that was in daylight, with guides that knew the area well, this was completely different. Mitch started after Elena in the direction he figured the sound was coming from. As he pushed through the underbrush he looked back and saw the lights of Teo, Louis, the students, Herman and Perez, and anyone else available coming. The lights were bouncing off the branches and leaves of the overhanging trees, lending a surreal glow to the already unreal scene.

Mitch stopped to yell to them, "Over here, come over here," and wave his arm uselessly in the direction he thought Elena had gone, but he had to keep moving or lose the sound of her passing.

Elena heard her pursuers also, and although she was still running she was beginning to calm down a little, shaking her head from side to side as if to shake off the awful knowledge she was beginning to accept, when she was hit in the face by a heavy branch with thorns on it. The blow knocked her down to her knees and she just settled back to a sitting position, holding her knees and crying, the bitter taste of the truth stuck in her throat. There was something wrong going on and her father was part of it. "Why had he worked so hard all these years only to throw it all away?" she asked herself bitterly, "Why couldn't those government bureaucrats had given us the money we needed in the first place?" What would happen if their friends and colleagues at the University found out? But she really didn't have to ask herself what would happen, because she already knew; she knew that both his career and his reputation would be destroyed, and she that if that happened then he would need her more than he ever did before. "And I'll never leave my father's side," she thought angrily. Now filled with resolve to stand by her father no matter what, she was shifting position to stand up, tasting her own blood that ran off her forehead when she felt the first bite.

"Oh, God," she thought, "Ants, the ants!" As she jumped up screaming and slapping she could feel that there were already hundreds of them on her, beneath her clothes, running up her arms, some crawling out her collar and onto her neck. "Help me, help me," she called out as she began running and jumping. "Ants, ants!" she screamed, not knowing which way the stream of ants was coming from but knowing that there were more and more of them and that her only chance was to keep moving. The twisting red-brown flow of the innumerable soldiers of the ant army was like a huge sinuous, sinister beast, made up of millions and millions of individual cells, each with eight legs and powerful jaws for biting, silently overwhelming and eating everything in their path.

When Mitch heard Elena's scream he shouted, "Over here," and madly pushed his way towards her. But when he felt the ants running up his pant legs his heart sank. He knew the ant's bite was very virulent and enough bites could kill a creature much larger than a man or woman. He kept moving, slapping at his legs as he yelled back to Teo and the rest of the would-be rescuers, GGo back, stay away from the ants!"

"No, no," replied Teo, panting, sweaty and scared, "We're coming too!"

"No!" Mitch shouted vehemently, "Go back to the road and use your lights to guide us back, hurry!" Then he turned and ran zig-zag through the trees like a running back because he could hear Elena screaming in agony. As he crashed headlong through the underbrush, using his hands and arms to try to fend off the branches and to keep the ants crawling up his neck off of his face, he remembered some of the rescues he had made in the surf off of Fort Lauderdale when he was a lifeguard. Then, as now, Mitch had been surprised that going into a dangerous situation or even facing possible death wasn't as hard as he always imagined it would be. Even though the heroes of the movies or books could face any kind of danger without flinching, Mitch felt that real courage involved having real fear but overcoming it, of acting without thought for yourself in spite of your fears. But whenever Mitch had been in that kind of situation before, there hadn't been any fear to overcome, because it was pushed to the back of his mind along with everything else not related to the situation at hand, as his actions were determined by training and adrenalin. He also knew from the time that he had reached out blindly while being tossed helplessly around under the water by the powerful and turbulent shore break over the sandbar, more or less thinking about saving his own ass at that point, when he snared the would-be victims ankle and wound up making the rescue, that you never gave up, no matter what. So he frantically ignored the ants swarming over his legs, climbing up into his armpits, biting his ears and around his eyes, and he just kept running madly through the jungle when suddenly the ground went out from under him and he found himself falling through the branches and splashing down in a pool of a shallow but wide creek. Crashing about ten feet through the air and landing face first in the water had dislodged many of the insects from his body and as he shot upright in the waist deep water he wiped more off his face and from around his eyes in time to see Elena come rolling down the side of the little gully, moaning in pain and covered with biting ants. She had gone as far as she could, just struggling to stay upright, blindly skirting the edge of the river of ants, until she just couldn't go anymore, raking with her hands at the ants on her face that were biting her near her eyes and mouth, when she fell forward onto her knees and then rolled right off the edge of the creek bed to the bank of the little stream, where a surprised but unquestioning Mitch grabbed her and pulled her into the water. She was barely conscious and delirious but too weak to struggle much and he held her, both of them crying, as he pulled off as many ants as he could from her slender body. His own face was beginning to puff up and he couldn't see very well but he knew the ants were all around them and he didn't know what to do. So he stayed in the middle of the pool and held Elena as the ants poured down both sides of the creek bed and pushed a foot or two out into the water before finally flowing around them and off into the jungle. Mitch still just stood there, feeling the strength ebb from his body and his consciousness getting fuzzy as the toxin from all the ant bites started going through his system. He could feel his feet going numb and his knees starting to tremble, but he didn't know if it was from the ant bites or the chill water of the stream moving gently against his legs and over Elena's ravaged form held desperately in front of him. As Mitch stood there swaying on the edge of consciousness, struggling to hold onto Elena and stay upright, his mind flashed back to the many scenes of the past few months, a quick burst of indelible memories, rolling by like a crazily edited movie, scenes like watching Elena stride away towards the kitchen of the Hotel Astoria the first time they met, her cute shorts and silly hat as they flirted among the ruins and relics on her father's tour, and of course her graceful, innocent beauty as she laughed over her shoulder at him while swimming naked across the pool by the waterfall during those wonderful, long last hours of languid, late afternoon sunlight just a little while ago. Even in his dazed state Mitch was struck by the irony of the same creek that had given them such a fertile place for their passion to grow as they clung to each other in the taken for granted strength of youth and health, was part of the same flow of the clear, cool lifeblood of the jungle that now gave their weak and battered bodies what they so desperately needed. Mitch remembered the glow her face had then, and when he looked at her now he knew she was in a bad way, her face all puffed up and her eyes swollen shut, her breathing shallow and irregular and now Mitch could see the goose bumps when she got the cold flashes that he was starting to feel. The jungle creek had given them their chance but now it was up to him if they were going to make it. Again Mitch didn't know exactly what to do, but he knew he didn't want to die right there, so he summoned up all his remaining strength and mental energy for a try for the bank. "Well, nothing for it but to get going," he thought as he lifted up Elena and tried to stumble to the bank. He had just managed to drag her to the edge of the water and was resting on his hands and knees when he heard voices and saw lights. "Over here . . . help," he tried to yell, but it came out more like a croak. Then it all got to be too much, the eerily bouncing lights, the cold, clammy feeling of his skin, the bites, Elena lying there so still beneath him, and he just let it go, passing out into the muddy bank and the complete dark of the jungle in his mind.

*   *   *

    Dr Comacho, sleeping fitfully in the house of one of the investors in Miami, suddenly sat straight up in bed, wide awake, with his fists clenched and every muscle of his body tensed to the point of cramping, drips of sweat running down his ribcage as he was gripped by a feeling of phantom panic, of over-whelming anxiety coming out of nowhere to jerk him out of his uneasy rest. He thought immediately of Elena and the dig, shaking his head and rubbing the back of his neck as he sought to clear his mind and relax a little, sighing deeply as he recognized where he was and sank back on the pillow. Even as he looked around the luxurious room, with its marble tile floors, beautiful original artwork, and heavy silk draperies framing a window with an incredible view of Biscayne Bay in the moonlight beyond an immaculately manicured garden, he couldn't get his worries about the dig and his people out of his mind. "All of this luxury is wasted on me," he thought ruefully, thinking back on the couple of days he had been there already. Even though Dr Comacho had never been poor, and the University provided him with a comfortable furnished apartment when he was teaching in the city, he just wasn't ready for the unbelievably opulent lifestyle of the moneyed elite of Miami. Dr Comacho had come from a fairly well off family himself, and he knew several very wealthy people through fund-raising for museum and University functions, but these people in Miami were different, not understated at all like most of the very rich, but almost flamboyant, as if they enjoyed the public display of their extravagance, as if they were engaged in some incredibly expensive game of one-upmanship. "What was that saying I saw on that bumper sticker of that Porche?" the Professor thought as he threw off the percale linen sheets trimmed in silk that matched the silk pajamas the maid had laid out after dinner, "The one who dies with the most toys wins?" The Professor peeled off his pajama top, now wet with anxious sweat, and threw it on the near-by Queen Anne chair as he walked to the center of the room to stand under the ceiling fan, feeling the hot, humid air coming in the open window reluctantly cooling him as it was forced over his half-naked body. Of course his room did have air-conditioning (there wouldn't be hardly anyone in Florida without it), but the Professor preferred real air, not filtered and processed air. Even if it meant sweating a little he enjoyed seeing the curtains move with the breeze, the smell of the salty air and the sound of the slap of the waves against the seawall, waves driven across the bay in ragged formation by the almost constant trade winds blowing over the Gulfstream from the Bahamas. He caught the beautifully sweet and delicate scent of the night-blooming Jasmine as he stepped over to the window and looked down the seawall at his host's ninety-four foot ocean-going yacht tied up at the private dock, all dark now except for a safety light on the radar mast, not quite quiet as it's lines creaked as they were stretched over the cleats and it's pennants rustled in the same breeze that cooled Dr Comacho behind the screen at the window. An ocean-going yacht, with a captain, a first mate, and an engineer, along with two crewmen, not counting the bartender and cocktail waitress who had come along, with the Captain and probably the mate making more per year than a full professor back in Mexico City, and they had used it just to cruise up the Intracoastal Waterway to have lunch at a private club on the water. But the Professor had to admit that despite their apparent wealth and obvious penchant for spending it, his hosts otherwise seemed to be quite reasonable and educated people. He thought of Enrique Bolina, the man who owned the villa where he was staying and the yacht he was looking at, the man who was Archetti's boss and was now one of the main sponsors of the Professor's project.

As a tanned and thin, neatly dressed gentleman somewhere in his early fifties, with his sophisticated manners balanced by his considerable friendly charm, Bolina moved with ease among the wealthy and powerful of the glittery Gold Coast of South Florida. Dr Comacho recalled seeing him standing on the bow of his million dollar boat with his arms folded, watching the performance of the hired help as the captain, standing way above Bolina on the bridge, coolly maneuvered the unwieldy booze cruiser gently up to the dock at the Horsemen's Club, to the delight of both Bolina and the several patron's at the patio bar who had been watching with lazy interest. Why the place was called the Horsemen's Club never became clear to Dr Comacho, because none of the people he met seemed to have anything to do with horses, except maybe to own a couple of stables or a polo team or two, but he felt better when he saw that Mr Bolina seemed to be admired and respected by everyone that he introduced the Professor to, whether they were Anglo or Latin, politician or businessman. Several of Bolina's friends were interested in archeology and were fairly well versed on the subject, and although their knowledge was probably due to the scholarly discipline's recent glamorization by Hollywood films and popular magazines, Dr Comacho wound up having a lively and enjoyable discussion with them as they went on their cruise to nowhere up and down the Intracoastal. He was also reassured to see how circumspect Rick Archetti acted when he was around Bolina or any of the other rich and influential members of Bolina's social set. Rick had been his usual confident self when he met Dr Comacho at the airport, with his Vaurnet sunglasses perched on his head, wearing a white linen jacket over a pastel yellow casual shirt unbuttoned almost to his navel, he led the thoroughly lost Dr Comacho to the long black Mercedes limo provided by his boss after greeting him with a cocky smile and a casual arm on his shoulder, but his attitude toned down rapidly as they pulled onto the grounds of Bolina's villa on the private island off of the causeway. It wasn't like Rick was being a toady and there wasn't even a hint of boot-licking about it, but he just tried to make himself as helpful and friendly as possible without really kissing anyone's ass. Just little things like going down the gangplank first to assist their guests when they had dropped them off back at the club, opening doors for the ladies and things like that, and bigger things, like not making a play for any of his boss's friend's ladies or never contradicting his boss or his boss's friends when they allowed him to join their discussions. "Then why does he act like such a jerk when he's on the dig?" the Professor thought as he slowly wandered back across the room and sat on the edge of the bed, "Oh, well, maybe when he gets out from under his bosses' noses he likes to play the big guy himself." Dr Comacho was relieved to see this side of Rick, though, because it made it easier for him to dismiss all of Rick's talk of Mexico City, of robbery, and his hints of danger in their enterprise as just so much macho posturing, probably more the result of Rick stroking his own ego than a calculated plan designed to impress them or to scare them into staying in line. Dr Comacho sighed and lay down on his back, using his feet to kick the rumpled top sheet out of the way as he tried to slow the rush of worries and anxieties cruising through his brain to the point where he could get some rest. He succeeded in putting most of his doubts about Rick and his bosses on hold in the back of his mind, but a persistent nagging anxiety about Elena and the dig; and Mitch and all the other good people who were being caught up in his problems refused to let go, causing him an almost physical pain as he tossed and turned on top of the luxurious bed in an unsuccessful attempt at sleep. He knew that he would feel better and rest easier in his shorts and old undershirt, lying on his shaky but reliable old cot in his mildewing tent in the jungle, but that didn't help him now, and neither did the persistent feeling deep down in his bones that he was needed there.

*   *   *

Things came to Mitch in bits and pieces for the rest of that terrible night. He felt strong arms picking him up as the rescuers, led by Perez and Herman, found him and Elena. They hadn't stayed back at the road but had come straight into the jungle behind the last of the river of ants, the plan being to hit the creekbed, which Herman and Perez knew to be in that area, and move along it calling their friend's names. Their reasoning was that the rescue party could move faster along the relatively clear banks of the creek than by pushing through the brush. The locals among them also knew, but didn't say, that if Mitch and Elena had any kind of chance it was in the water. They knew if they didn't find them along the creekbed, then they would probably never find them at all. So there was much cheering when they were first spotted sprawled in the mud together, but it quickly turned to urgent questions and murmured prayers when the rescuers could see how badly Mitch and Elena had been hurt. Those among them who were bitten by the stragglers of the ant army as they picked up the victims were consumed by a heart-felt sympathy for Elena and Mitch, whose bodies were covered with bites. Mitch felt the cool breeze coming down the road raise goosebumps on his already puffy and swollen skin. Fuzzily through his nearly closed eyelids he could see the faces of his friends and hear the urgency in their voices as they put him and Elena into the back of the pick-up truck for the ride into town. He was not really conscious, but he knew they were in serious trouble, that it wasn't over yet. He tried to sit up as Teo was tucking a blanket over him, trying to make his swollen lips and thickening tongue say the words to his question, but all that came out was a whispered, gasping,"Elena . . .?" Mitch slipped in and out of awareness as he felt his body twisting and jerking as it banged against the sides and bed of the pick-up truck, but most of his more lucid moments were spent in a kind of eerie, detached state in which he had the impression of being a coolly unaffected observer, hovering somewhere between the truck's bed and cab as he calmly watched the hurried, desperate actions of his friends as they tried to cover him for the run into town. His attention slid over to the mostly still form of Elena covered by blankets in the bed of the pick-up next to his thrashing body; whether it was because she was smaller than him or had been bitten more times, he couldn't guess, but she seemed much more far gone than he was, being already deeply unconscious, moving only when a spasm flowed down her poisoned body like a wave or to rub her swollen shut eyes and distended lips into the rolled up sweater that someone had put under her head for a pillow as she mumbled incoherently or coughed weakly. Mitch wanted with all his being to be able to reach out to her, to hold her and comfort her, but he couldn't, he could only observe as his body continued it's uncontrolled writhing under the blankets his friends had wrapped tightly around him. "So this is what it's like to die," he thought calmly as he felt a great fatigue settling over him. He thought it was strange that he felt no fear, no panic or great foreboding, just a strong sense of regret when he looked down at his battered and swollen body. He knew he wasn't a teenager anymore, and he knew he had picked up his share of nicks and dings over the years but it still seemed as awful shame to waste such a serviceable body that probably had a lot of good days left. He remembered getting the same feeling when he had seen his grandfather's body lying still on the kitchen floor, after he had died quietly in the night while going for a midnight snack. He remembered bending down and closely looking over the remains, seeing no signs of distress on the outside and yet knowing that this wasn't like a used car, where you could just replace the parts that had gone bad and get it going again. "On, well, I guess I'll be seeing him again soon," he thought in a final attempt at cool nonchalance as he fought off the feelings of lethargy and exhaustion washing over him and struggled to stay awake. Mitch felt the bouncing of the truck smooth out a little as they pulled into town and he felt himself being picked up again and placed on a stretcher. He felt the local Doctor's strong fingers on his arm as the Doctor gave them both a shot of antihistamine and ant anti-toxin, but that was about it. He couldn't talk and he couldn't stay conscious long enough to find out about Elena, and finally he just slid over into the abyss and sank into the total darkness of near coma.

Chapter Nine: Confession

The next few days were a nightmare for Mitch. He had awakened in a hospital room in the capital, the antiseptic whiteness of the room and the bright sunlight coming in the window hurt his eyes as he looked through the narrow slits in his still puffy face. Teo and Louis were there and they told him how the military people had radioed the capital and how the plane that flew the few tourists to the ruins had come out and picked them up. They had left Herman and Perez in charge of the dig and then had jumped in the plane with him and Elena. They excitedly told him how terrifying it had been, not so much the night take-off from the narrow airstrip in the jungle or the maniacal screaming of the siren as the ambulance raced from the airport to the hospital, as the dread fear that their friends were dying, and of the frustration of being helpless, unable to do anything but wait and hope. They told how he and Elena had arrived at the hospital in critical condition and were taken to the intensive care unit where they were put on an intravenous solution of anti-toxin, the medical staff here crediting the quick and correct action of the small town doctor with probably saving their lives. Teo and Louis had watched dumbly as Mitch and Elena, wrapped in white sheets and surrounded by medical personnel, were hustled away on gurneys, disappearing into an elevator within minutes of arriving at the hospital. After they had anxiously shepherded their unconscious friends through the emergency room procedures and stuck around to answer what questions they could about Mitch's and Elena's health history, age, and the like for the concerned staff doctors, Teo and Louis had finally, as the weak, gray light of dawn eased in through the emergency room windows, been persuaded to go to find a place to get some rest. As they stepped out of the artificial environment of the hospital and into the early morning hustle of the city streets, with the ever present tinge of diesel smoke in the air, the shouting of the men and the banging of the trays as the hospital workers unloaded the trucks bringing the food and supplies for that day, both Louis and Teo experienced a strange feeling of disorientation, a kind of emotional jet-lag or severe culture shock. Going from being pleasantly tired after a good days work in the isolated and seemingly endless jungle in the evening to stumbling along exhausted down the busy thoroughfares of the large, modern city the next morning was almost too much for their battered psyches to bear. They started out in a kind if a daze, not saying much but just sort of sub-consciously steering a course away from the steel and glass towers of the downtown center towards the older section of town surrounding it, looking for a pension or hotel nearby to get "un quarto por la noche"; a room for the night. They both would have preferred to go back to the Hotel Astoria, because it seemed a familiar and reassuring place in their minds just then, but it was all the way across town and they wanted to stay close to the hospital so they found a place the way they usually did; by asking other backpackers. They had only gone a couple of blocks away from the hospital when they came upon one of the many plazas, which were like tiny mini-parks dotted all over the old colonial sections of the city, maybe a block square, usually fronted by a huge Catholic church or a government building, with large, old trees shading rows of benches, and manicured lawns and hedges intersected by wide sidewalks, usually with a statue or fountain or maybe a band shell type gazebo in the center. These plazas were filled with vendors and artists, musicians and shoppers, retirees and tourists, worshippers from the church and workers from the surrounding buildings coming down to eat their lunches out of doors and watch the people go by. It didn't take long for Teo and Louis to spot a young couple, obviously American, sitting on a bench rearranging their packs in order to stuff in the hammocks they had just bought from a street vendor. The guys just paused long enough to make eye contact and say hi and then strolled over and struck up a conversation. It was never hard to talk to fellow travelers on the gringo trail because meeting interesting people and exchanging stories was one of the main reasons why many of the backpackers were even out there, and anyway, being asked for information makes most people feel important, especially if they know the answer to the question. This young couple, "Jay and Kelly from Houston, Texas", was the way they introduced themselves, listened with mounting interest and sympathy as Louis told them an abbreviated version of the story of the dig and what had happened to Mitch and Elena out in the jungle. When Louis finished they jumped up and insisted on not just telling them where their pension, the Dolores Alba, was, but also on leading them there, happy to be even a small part of an honest-to- God adventure. The Dolores Alba was similar to the Astoria, except that here the cook, la cochina, was also the owner, a middle-aged widow who ran the dozen room hotel with the help of an elderly

aunt and two teenage nieces. The Dolores Alba
would have been an easy place to miss, the
only clue that there was a hotel behind the tall,
wooden stable doors along a city street lined
with the back walls of buildings whose
entrances were on the other block was the
name, Dolores Alba, painted in red letters on
the dingy white wall above the double doors,
which looked old enough to have swung open
for horse drawn carriages in their day. But once
you came inside those old doors the Alba was
actually a very cozy place to stay, being above
average in that each room had a private bath,
and there was a beautiful enclosed courtyard
centered by a spreading banyan tree with a pet
monkey tied to it's base, and even a small,
walled-in swimming pool up on the back patio.
But the only feature of the Alba that Teo and
Louis availed themselves of was the free
breakfast of fruit, bread and eggs served each
morning by the proprietress, before they went
off to the hospital where they spent almost all
their time, waiting. On the third day they
arrived early to find that Mitch, having come
back to consciousness first, had been moved

down one floor to the regular wards, being considered past the crisis and on the road to recovery. Elena, on the other hand, remained in intensive care, even though she regained consciousness about twelve hours after Mitch did. Dr Comacho had of course been contacted in Miami, the morning after his sleepless night, and he immediately flew back, arriving the evening after the terrible incident had occurred. He spent every minute he was allowed to next to Elena's bed the whole two and a half days that she was unconscious. He was tremendously relieved and he broke into tears of joy and gratitude when she finally regained consciousness, but he was confused and hurt when all she would say was that she didn't want to see anyone. The doctors at first had put her slow recovery down to her smaller size and the tremendous number of bites all over her body, but now they were clearly worried by her lack of improvement. While Mitch had recovered enough to hobble painfully about the hospital and was getting back his appetite for solid food, Elena remained in bed on intravenous feeding, making no effort to get up. She would just lie in bed, holding her father's hand, looking into his eyes with tears running down her cheeks, but she would only shake her head slowly from side to side when he would try to reassure her, tell her everything would be all right. Dr Comacho was frantic with worry, starting to look like he did during the early days of the dig when things weren't going too well. He had been down to see Mitch, and Mitch had been shocked to see how haggard he looked, as if he had taken the ills of his daughter on his own body. They had talked and the Professor told Mitch that everything was fine at the dig and that he was happy that Mitch was going to be ok. They talked about what had happened in the jungle, but not how it had happened or why. Mitch was worried about how much to tell him and when, because he thought that Elena would want to ask her father about the situation first, so he sort of skirted the issue, afraid of what he would have to say if confronted. But Dr Comacho was clearly distracted by his concern for his daughter and he didn't press Mitch about it. He had stayed long enough to be polite, and then went back to Elena's room, leaving Mitch to worry and wait.

One morning early the next week Dr Jaime Gonzalez Alvaro de Medina ran his hand through his thick black hair, tinged with gray streaks that had come pretty early to a man not yet thirty-five, and shook his head as he stood at the counter of the nurse's station filling out his latest report on Elena's condition. "How is she doing, Doctor?" the nurse behind the counter asked as she took the report from him to file it.   "She's not progressing like she should, but, the truth is," he continued, "I'm more worried about the father than the patient at this point."

"Oh, really," the nurse replied, looking up attentively, fishing for that one good tidbit of gossip that would be all over the hospital by that evening, "Why, because he looks so tired?"

"Well," Dr Alvaro started to answer but he let it drop when he noticed Dr Comacho leave Elena's room and approach the station. Even though Dr Comacho looked thoroughly exhausted, gaunt, pale, and even a little unsteady on his feet, Dr Alvaro could see the purposefulness and maybe a little anger in his eyes as he met Dr Alvaro's glance and raised one finger to signal to Dr Alvaro to wait and talk to him. "Oh, no," Dr Alvaro thought as he shuffled his papers uneasily, "What am I going to tell him?" He knew that Dr Comacho hadn't been sleeping much or eating right for the last few days, but it was more than that, it was obvious to him that Dr Comacho had been under stress for more than just a few days. "He is going to want to know why his daughter is not getting better as quickly as she should," he thought anxiously, a little aggravated now himself, "Well, I'd like to know what's going on here, too." He knew Dr Comacho spent a lot of time with Elena, but they didn't seem to talk much, and what about the gringo downstairs? From what Dr Alvaro had heard he had been some kind of hero, getting himself all bitten up trying to help Senorita Comacho, but ever since they were brought in together she refused to see him. "Now what is this shit?" he mused, turning away slightly as Dr Comacho joined him at the counter, "She'll see her father, and he goes to see the gringo, but neither the gringo or his friends can go see her, even though he apparently saved her life!" Dr Jaime Gonzalez Alvaro de Medina was a dedicated doctor who worked very hard and he was just as concerned and frustrated as Dr Comacho that Elena wasn't responding as she should, and he wasn't about to take any guff about it.

"Dr Alvaro, I need to talk to you for a minute," Dr Comacho started out sternly, "Is there a problem with Elena that I don't know about? I mean she doesn't seem to be, ah, I mean, ah, well Mitch is already . . ."

"You mean why isn't she getting better?" Dr Alvaro shot back, arching his eyebrows and looking directly into Dr Comacho's eyes, "Why don't you tell me?" Dr Comacho was a professor, not a medical doctor, and he had been pretty uncomfortable with even appearing to question Dr Alvaro's competence, but he was definitely surprised and confused by the vehemence of his response.

"What do you mean?" Dr Comacho

stammered out weakly, "If there was anything I could tell you, any thing I could do to help, let me know, I'll do it." Dr Alvaro looked up at that haggard face, so full of pain, and felt instantly sorry for the way he had reacted. He reached out and put his hand on Dr Comacho's forearm.

"You don't know, do you?" he asked gently, and then went on, "Well, we know that Elena was attacked by the army ants that night in the bush, and we know they hurt her on the outside, but something else happened, something that hurt her on the inside, something that we can't cure with any kind of intravenous solution." He paused and waited while an agitated Dr Comacho desperately searched his memory for something, some incident that might have upset Elena, a gnawing guilt starting to cause a ball of pain in his gut. Dr Alvaro went on softly, "Look, she's young and healthy and she will recover completely anyway, but maybe if she wasn't depressed she would get better quicker. As a matter of fact, I'm sure of it." Then he said reassuringly, "Why don't you talk to her, or," here he paused and looked down toward Mitch's floor, "Talk to her boyfriend and his friends." Dr Comacho stood up straight with renewed energy and reached out to shake Dr Alvaro's hand,

"Thank you very much, Doctor, you have helped me a lot and I think that you are doing a great job." He turned away toward the elevator with a determined look on his face, saying, "I think I will have that talk with the guys, and right now!" Dr Alvaro turned back to the still attentive nurse and smiled; they both felt better now, Dr Alvaro because he had gotten all that off his chest with Dr Comacho, and the nurse because she had gotten her juicy tidbit of gossip after all.

That same morning Mitch, Teo and Louis were in Mitch's room discussing their situation. Mitch sat in a chair by the window, the warmth of the sun feeling good on his still pock-marked but no longer swollen face. Louis and Teo sat on the same side of the bed, Teo's feet on the floor and Louis's swinging under the bed as they both leaned forward to speak in urgent near whispers.

"We have got to talk to Dr Comacho, Mitch" Teo said, "We have got to give him his chance to explain."

"Yeah, I want to know if there is any point to going back to the dig at all, if he is going to sell everything," declared Louis.

"He wasn't selling everything," retorted Teo, "Besides, we never would have gotten anywhere without that money."

"True, Teo," replied Mitch, "But what about Elena? Do we tell him that she knows, or should we wait for her to resolve it herself?" He knew Elena was still in bed, out of physical danger, her strong young body responding in spite of herself, but still not improving quickly or trying to.

"Yeah, but we can't even talk to her if she won't see us," mused Teo despondently. Just then Dr Comacho came striding into the room, his back straight and his eyes burning with anger. When the startled guys tried to mumble hello he held his hand up for silence like the teacher he was. He fixed a hard stare on Mitch's eyes and said,

"I have just been having a talk with

Elena's doctor. He said something happened that night that traumatized her emotionally, as well as physically, something that has taken away her motivation to get well." He paused and looked at the three in turn, searching their faces, Teo and Louis breaking his stare and looking down at their feet, but Mitch stared defiantly back into his eyes. "Now I want to know just what the hell was going on out there and I want to know now!" the Professor shouted, raising his fist above his head, looking like some kind of wild man, with the dark circles under his eyes the dominate feature of his pale face.

"No," Mitch shouted back, jumping up from the chair, "You tell us what's going on, Professor!" Mitch scraped his chair back violently and stepped forward so that he was right in the Professor's face and whispered vehemently, "You tell us, Doctor, because we're the ones who hauled the supplies, cut the trees, dug in the mud and the bugs and the heat for those artifacts just so you could sell them!" Dr Comacho's face went instantly white and he seemed to shrink like an inner-tube with a slow leak as he sighed deeply and sat down on the edge of the bed, thinking how it definitely wasn't his day for confrontations. "How . . .?" he said weakly as he looked up at Mitch's angry face. "We followed you, we saw you and Rick and Miguel in the warehouse, so you tell us," Mitch demanded again. The Professor sat bent over on the bed, with his forearms on his thighs, his head hung down staring at his hands hanging limply between his knees, and said in a low voice,

"Well, what . . . I mean did you look in the window, did you go down into the basement . . ?"

"It's no use, Dr Comacho," retorted Mitch emphatically, "We were right in the warehouse with you, and we heard you making a deal with Rick."

"But why did you follow me?" asked Dr Comacho, "I thought we were friends." Teo and Louis had stood up when Dr Comacho sat down and now the three guys shifted uncomfortably as they stood over the Professor.

"Well," Teo began hesitantly, "We were all wondering about the money and these private investors, . . . and Mitch doesn't like Mr Archetti very much."

Dr Comacho looked up at Mitch, "You are showing good judgment, my gringo amigo, I'm not sure I like him much myself ...although for different reasons I'm sure." He smiled at Teo and Louis and said, "This brings us back to Elena. I suppose she found out?" Teo broke in before Mitch could reply,

"Yes, but we didn't accuse you of anything, ah, we wanted to wait and give you a chance to explain." He paused and glanced nervously at Dr Comacho and then his friends, "I was, ah, that is, we were sure you had a good reason for what you were doing, but Elena just, ah, . . ." The Professor got up as Teo mumbled to a halt and Mitch took over for him,

"We weren't going to say anything until we talked to you, but she found out that we followed you and confronted us with it. We told her what we had seen, without making any conclusions, but she didn't believe us and that is when she ran into the bush." Mitch looked questioningly at the Professor, "She hasn't talked to you about it?" he asked.

"No," replied Dr Comacho, "But I guess it's time she did, right? Come on, guys, let's go get this is out in the open right now!" With that he turned and walked out, leaving the guys to hurry after him.

*   *   *

Elena swung her legs over the side of the bed and slid carefully down until her feet hit the floor, and stood up slowly and then walked listlessly over to the window to stand in the bright morning sunlight streaming in. She felt a little dizzy so she leaned against the windowsill, feeling the warmth of the sun's rays on her still sensitive but healing skin. And despite the real physical battering her body had taken and all her emotional turmoil, Elena realized that she was starting to develop a bad case of cabin fever. "Hospitals have a way of doing that to you," she thought as she wandered slowly across the room back to the bed. She picked up the pitcher of ice water on

the little table next to the bed and started to
pour some into her plastic cup when she
noticed that the cup was already half full. She
shrugged and filled it up anyway, then drank it
back down to halfway and left it there. She
sighed as she swung her hips back up on the
bed and sat half upright against the pillows, her
feet kicking off the tangled topsheet with quick,
irritated motions. She still felt like she was at an
emotional impasse and she hated the
uncertainty of not knowing what to do, but she
also knew that her body and her mind were
missing the constant and satisfying activities if
the dig and that she would go crazy if she had
to stay around here much longer. She slid down
the bed to lie almost flat and flexed every
muscle in her body, starting with her head and
going all the way down until her toes were
pointed and cramping with effort, then running
her hands over her tight hips and firm, slender
thighs. She had lost some weight and most of
her color during her stay in the hospital, and
she knew that many of the ant bites had left
little scars on her but she also knew that she
was young and that with some time and a good

tan they wouldn't be that noticeable. She still felt attractive, even sexy. She squirmed around in the bed and reached down to pull the topsheet back over her, a little angry at herself when she realized that all this attention to her body had made her think of Mitch, remembering how alive she had felt when she was with him. "How can I think about that son-of-a-bitch after what he said about my father?"she groused to herself as she let her head flop down on the pillow in frustration,"Why can't we just . . ." Elena sat upright in surprise as just then the four of them marched into her room, Dr Comacho at the head of the little group, with Mitch to his left, slightly behind, and Teo and Louis behind them. She settled back down to a half sitting, reclining position against her pillow, her eyes slipping from face to face as the Professor spoke to the nurse, getting her to leave the room. "What's going on?"Elena thought uncertainly, questions starting to spin in her mind,"Why are they all together, doesn't my father know what they are accusing him of?" She was so confused, hating Mitch for calling her father a liar and a thief, yet full of her own questions and doubts. The two men she cared about most in the world were playing tug-of-war with her trust and it was tearing her apart. Long after the pain of the ant bites and her broken skin had faded the ache in her heart and the frustration in her mind had kept her from a minutes rest or comfort. All these days her father had sat with her, holding her hand, telling her that he loved her and that everything would be all right, she was hating herself for what she was thinking, for even having such questions in her mind. But they wouldn't go away and she couldn't bring herself to put them into words. Now her father and Mitch were here in her room, together. "Maybe it's out in the open now," she thought apprehensively as she watched them arrange themselves around the room, Teo and Louis standing at the foot of the bed, Mitch leaning back against the windowsill, and her father coming to her side and taking her hand.

"Daughter," he began with his head bowed and a choke in his voice, "I'm here to

explain everything, and to beg your forgiveness
. . ."

"No, no, Papa," Elena said as she sat upright again, "It's them," she said, pointing to Mitch and the guys, "They are not your friends, they ..." With that she trailed off, looking up at her father, still unable to repeat their accusations to him. Mitch had met her angry lightning bolt of a look firmly but he was actually relieved to see such energy in her eyes. And Mitch was more than just mentally aware of her presence in the room as he felt a shot of adrenalin run up his spine and get his heart pumping and his hands sweating as he met the still smoldering anger in her eyes. It was more like his body could physically feel her energy, whether through some kind of ESP mind wave or simply his subconscious mind using all the subtle capabilities of the five senses to get bits of information that the conscious mind is too cluttered and confused to recognize or process, things like the tiny squeak of the hospital white sheets under her hip as she shifted around to sit up, the light but definite touch of her warm, human scent against the chemical tinge of the hospital air, or the miniature lightshow caused by the late morning sunlight refracting off the tiny golden-clear hairs running down the side of her delicate neck. He had been shocked when they first came in to see how small and frail she looked, lying there with her head on a huge looking white pillow, her shiny black hair highlighting the paleness of her face. But when Mitch saw the fire in her eyes, he knew that she still had her strength inside, and that the old Elena would return to them. It was then he allowed himself to see her beauty, the darkness of her hair and eyebrows accenting her high cheekbones and her dark Indian eyes, now looking questioningly at Dr Comacho as he said,

"No, my daughter, you are wrong, they are friends, good friends," he turned and pulled a chair up to the edge of the bed, "Now, no more interruptions, just let me explain and get this off my chest." The Professor went on to tell the story that Mitch and the guys had already guessed at. He told of how hard it had been to find funds in this country, how the government had given them nothing but promises, of his frustration of knowing the dig was an important one and seeing how hard his people had to work to make progress that would have been easy with the right equipment. Then he spoke of the contrast between that and the obvious wealth of the private investors he had met through some friends at the museum in Miami. They had him out to their estates to show him their collections and had entertained him lavishly, even though he told them that the artifacts that he was finding were of great historical significance to his country and would never leave it. He had first gotten into trouble when he had accepted some of their financial aid with "no strings attached". It was that way in the beginning, he said, but when he saw how much better the work went, how much more solid progress they could make, he knew he couldn't stop taking the money. He started thinking about the investor's repeated requests for anything, any unimportant piece that wasn't essential to the scholarship of the dig. When Elena heard this she protested,

"No, Papa, every piece is unique and important and we can't give anything up!" But the Professor replied,

"Well, daughter, then we may have had to give everything up. The dig wasn't going too well at all, and you yourself have seen how much more work we have been able to do since we have had some funding. I just thought it was worth it to give up a little to make so much more progress and get out so many more artifacts."

"But what about your reputation if you get found out, Papa?" asked Elena with tears in her eyes, "What about the exhibit you were going to take on the lecture circuit?" The Professor took both of her hands in his as he said,

"I apologize most to you, Elena, but I want you to understand that I felt I had no choice, that I was backed into a corner. Most of my reputation is tied to this dig anyway; if the dig fails I will be unable to reach the young people of this country and teach them about their heritage. And actually we are keeping the really important pieces for ourselves and we will have a very impressive exhibit when we finish on the dig." The Professor stopped and stood up, still holding one of Elena's hands, and looked slowly around the group, making eye contact with each in turn before saying, "And that's what we are going to do, right? Finish the dig, keep working toward our goals, stick together. I would like to know now who is with me." With that he stood in front of Mitch and extended his hand. "Mitch?" he said expectantly and waited. Mitch hesitated, hoping the uneasy feeling he had inside didn't show on his face as he calmly looked at Dr Comacho.

"Why don't I feel good about this?" he grumbled in his thoughts," is it just me? Maybe I really am too paranoid." He could see that Teo and Louis felt good about the reconciliation and that Elena wanted it badly, perhaps even needed it, and he wanted to feel good about it too, and he was a little irritated that he didn't. He thought of Elena; he certainly didn't want to put her through any more emotional turmoil, knowing that there was no way his tiny unidentifiable doubts were worth risking her health anymore. "And what about Dr Comacho?" Mitch thought as he looked directly into the man's eyes, DR Comacho returning his stare calmly and firmly, "What do I want from him?" When the man had come clean, confessed his sins, bared his soul in front of them, begged for and won his daughter's forgiveness, who was Mitch to continue to question him? Oh, well," Mitch sighed inwardly as he sort of settled his thoughts, "I guess you have to trust somebody sometime." There was a long moment as Mitch looked around at everyone and then reached slowly for Dr Comacho's hand, hesitating a few inches away as he said, "Well, if Elena thinks it's okay, then it's okay by me." Then there was much laughter and more than one pair of teary eyes as the Professor was pulled off balance between Mitch's handshake and Elena jumping up and grabbing him in a hug around his neck. She buried her face in his shoulder, and sobbed,

"Yes, Papa, yes, I understand, I forgive you, I love you!" The Profeesor sighed and sat down on the bed, his arm still around Elena, and said,

"Good, maybe now we can get back to work."

*   *   *

`Things pretty much got back to normal at the dig after Elena got out of the hospital. Teo and Louis had accompanied a still weak and shaky Mitch on his trip back a few days before Elena was released. On the way to the capital airport (no one chose to ride the bus again), Mitch smiled at Teo and said, Hey, this is great, let's spend some of Rick's bosses' money. Sure beats riding that damn bus, right?"

"You haven't seen the landing strip yet, Mr Macho," replied Teo laughing, "You'll be wishing you were on that bus when we go in to land."

"Yeah, well, anything has to be better than that damn bus. At least with a plane you die quick," put in Louis, grinning. Then his face went serious as he looked at both guys and said, "We ought to stop talking about the money, ok? I mean we ought to just keep things to ourselves, right?"

"All right," replied Mitch, "I was just kidding around. You're right, Louis, we should just keep our heads down and do our jobs, ok?"

Their flight over the jungle was uneventful but Mitch still got gooseflesh a couple of times when he looked out the window and thought about all the millions and billions of ants marching around down there. The landing also made him grip the arms of his seat as he looked down at the white gash in the green carpet of jungle that made up the small runway. The strip was no wider than a small road and although the brush had been cleared away on the sides there were no shoulders. Mitch was torn between following the landing or admiring the magnificent view of the cleared ruins that the tourists got. It was incredible to see the towering tops of the massive pyramids rising out of the ocean of green around them, their manicured grounds and neat tour paths in stark contrast with the tangled and teeming plant life crowding in on them. As the plane descended to the narrow strip Mitch could see other mounds, constructions of man that had been reclaimed by the jungle, with trees and vines growing right out of solid rock. Mitch wondered what knowledge, what secrets they might contain, what kind of intrigues or adventures would have to happen to get that ancient knowledge to modern light. "It hasn't been easy in our case so far," mused Mitch as he watched the pilot line it up perfectly and then start standing on the brakes almost as soon as the wheels toughed down. He got it stopped about fifty yards from the end of the runway, and then turned around to taxi to the little shed that served as fuel depot and hanger. When the guys got off the plane, after shaking hands with the pilot, they were met by Herman and Perez, who had been faithfully keeping things going at the dig. There was a lot of grinning and slapping of backs when they saw Mitch and concerned questions about Elena once their first excitement had died down. On the way back to camp they told Mitch that Rick Archetti had been at the dig and had also gone to see Miguel in the village, but after that he had left, saying he would be back when the Professor and Elena returned. Teo asked how the work was going and Perez said that the graduate students had handled most of it and that he and Herman had just tried to keep the camp supplied and everything seemed to be going pretty good.

Three days after Mitch got out of the hospital the Professor and Elena made a triumphant return to the archeological site. Elena still looked a little pale, but she had regained her positive attitude and was eager to get back to work. The graduate students were happy to have her back, glad to lay down some of the responsibilities they had taken on during her absence, and also because they could tell that the tense feelings that had permeated the project for weeks were gone. Everyone associated with the expedition participated in the general feeling of relief, that things were ok, those that knew everything that was going on and those who knew nothing. Teo and Louis threw themselves into the work at the dig, Herman and Perez did the things that have to be done to keep the camp in operation, and Elena ran the inventory from the shade of her small tent set up at the dig, and Dr Comacho and Mitch were everywhere, separately and together. The Professor was more like his old self again, working down in the pit, getting sunburned and dirty and scraped and loving every minute of it. It really seemed as if a great weight had been lifted off his shoulders now that the deception was over. Mitch had watched him for a while but actually spent most of his time paying attention to Elena. He worried that she was working too much, or had gotten too much sun, whether she had eaten enough at breakfast or whether the topical lotion the doctor had given them was working. Elena scolded him for neglecting his work but she allowed herself to be the object of his concern and didn't seem to mind too much. There were many winks and nudges among the grad students when Mitch would walk Elena to the dinner tent in the evening, with his arms around her shoulders or holding her hand. Thoughts of their conflict and of the ants or Rick Archetti were a million miles from Mitch's mind, as he gratefully went through the days working and healing and thinking about Elena.

But one day the Professor brought him back to reality when he said, "Well, Mitch, I have heard from our people in Miami, it's time to get back at it. We have to pick up Rick at the airstrip and we can take this latest group of artifacts that Elena has catalogued to Miguel's on the way in, okay?"

"Sure, Prof," Mitch replied, "I'll get the truck and Herman and Perez to load it. Do you want one of them to come along to help unload?"

"No, I think you and I can handle it," Dr Comacho said quickly, "And anyway, with Rick and his gear they would have to ride in the back on the return trip." Mitch had to admit that that made sense but he also had to wonder why he was starting to feel uneasy again.

Chapter Ten: Conspiracy

In spite of Mitch's foreboding, the presence of Rick Archetti did little to disrupt the pleasant regimen of the expedition or the extremely pleasant progress of Mitch's relationship with Elena. When Rick had first seen Mitch and Elena come into the dinner tent together he smiled to himself, amused by the affectations of their obvious infatuation, but when he stood up to greet Elena he did so with what to Mitch was surprising courtesy and grace. What Mitch didn't know was that the possibility of a backwoods tryst with the naïve daughter of an even more naïve professor was just a diversion to Rick compared to the fast-lane life he lived back in Miami. He was getting tired of these trips to the jungle anyway. When it had first started it was pretty exciting, flying in and out, controlling the money, seeing if he could turn the Professor to their ends, but now it was getting to be just a pain in the ass. He didn't like having to leave his drugs and his guns behind, and he missed his tuned-up BMW sedan. He loved driving around on South Florida's highways, watching the working jerks looking at him as he passed them by in their older sedans and pick-up trucks. The old rednecks and construction workers were bad enough but the ones that really disgusted him were the middle-aged and older dudes trying to look sharp in silly pork-pie hats and sport jackets in the Florida heat, cruising from bar to racetrack to bar to jai-alai in aging Coupe-de-villes, Rivieras, and Toranados, small time losers trying to act like the Godfather, always just one scam away from making the big score. Rick always gave them his favorite "Fuck you" look as he passed them up, cutting off their smoking dinosaurs with his thirty thousand dollar ultra-modern, high tech ride, disliking them mainly because the reminded him of his father, a continually unemployed and alcoholic gambler and petty thief who taught his son nothing but how to lie, cheat, and steal. He only bothered to hang around his family at all when he didn't have any "action" going and was broke, which was a lot of the time, probably more than Rick's mother would have liked. He would just track them down to one of their depressing series of shabby little apartments, try to get on welfare or unemployment, take what little money Rick's mother may have had, then spend his time drinking beer, watching television and bullying his old lady and kid around. He believed that a man's home was his castle, whether he was the one paying for it or not. With Rick he alternated between trying to impress him with stories about the big deals he had done or was going to do, and trying to get the respect he couldn't get any other way by physically intimidating the boy, slapping him on the side of the head or kicking him in the butt, hard. It didn't make Rick respect him, just hate him, and Rick hated him even when he came around when he was on a roll, after one of his infrequent wins at jai-alai or some scam and would give Rick some money or a present, like a radio or something, because Rick knew he would just take it back later, to try to pawn it when he went broke like he always did. He would try to buy back Rick's affection cheaply but he never gave anything to his wife, no matter how big he had scored. The only things he had ever given her were a lot of grief, some bruises, and an unwanted baby. She was a wan, pallid, unhealthy looking woman, weak in both flesh and spirit, who, as Rick found out at an early age, was both a part-time prostitute and a full time drug addict.   Still, even an addicted mother sometimes loves her little baby and she tried pretty hard by her standards to provide her son some semblance of home life, pushing her thin, always weary body slowly around the kitchen in a dirty old robe, overcooking his eggs and burning his toast, telling him to "Eat it all, breakfast is the most important meal of the day" at least three times a week. But whenever Rick's father would come home in a drunken rage and start to knock her around, call her a whore and demand money, she would just whine and whimper and cower from him, and then give him whatever money they had, whether she had already promised to buy Rick something with it or not. He hated her for her cowardice, for caving in so easily every time, and he resented her giving up money and things he felt were rightfully his. He resented it and he took it out on her by treating her almost exactly the same way his father did, dominating her mentally as a young boy, and physically just as soon as he was big enough. They came to a kind of amiable, apathetic parting of the ways when Rick was about fifteen or sixteen, with her going on in her constant daze and Rick coming home less and less often, until he just didn't go back at all. Rick's father didn't care that his little family had dissolved, although he presumably kept track of his old lady to prey on her whenever he felt like it, but Rick never saw either one of them again, didn't know if they were alive or dead and didn't give a damn either way. Probably as a reaction to the dress and lifestyle of his father and his cronies, a group of schemers, gamblers and neighborhood bar bullshit artists, who were either stupidly loyal to the urban fashions of the Northeastern corridor "back home", wearing black shoes, black pants and a jacket in South Florida's sweltering heat, or wore what they mistakenly perceived to be the fashion statement of the tropics, the polyester leisure suit, with white shoes and a white belt, and a flower print shirt open to the chest[so everyone could see your gold chains] and the sleeves rolled back over the cuffs, Rick went the opposite way, carefully staying in the forefront of the fashion trends and just naturally gravitated to the money end of town, the many marinas and private docks lining the bay. He haunted the municipal marina, wearing the right clothes, doing any job, washing down boats or volunteering to help in the well deck of local charters, working with the lines and baits, and he eventually became kind of a free-lance mate, learning fishing, boating, and how to work for rich people. He hung around and was in the right place at the right time during the wide open, boom times for smuggling in the late seventies, a time when a lot of balls and a little luck was often enough to get you through. He made his way up the organization, made several daring runs as a captain bringing in reefer, and felt like he was doing pretty good for himself until Mr Bolina had made him his lieutenant and protégé, and Rick had seen what real money meant. Bolina, through several dummy corporations, owned the Sportfisherman that Rick had so proudly brought across the Gulfstream, and although he never got near the product or any work, he made twenty times Rick's pay, which Rick had considered a small fortune when he first got it. So Rick had seized upon this man as a role model, seeing him now as both a mentor and a potential rival, for Rick fully intended to be as rich and powerful as Bolina one day. That's why he didn't feel like he needed to compete with Mitch over Elena, because he felt so superior to Mitch in every way, and if it came down to a head to head confrontation between them, he knew he would have the advantage, if only in the element of surprise. "Oh, well," he thought,

"Let's get this thing moving. I'm ready to get out of here." With that he got up and excused himself, and headed down towards the Professor's tent.

As he approached the tent flap opened and the Professor stepped out.

"Hello, Rick," Dr Comacho said, smiling, "Nice evening, isn't it?"

"Yes, it sure is, Professor," replied Archetti, who then said, "Doc, I've got to talk to you . . ."

"Okay," broke in the Professor," we can talk on the way to the dining tent and over dinner, yes?"

"Well, actually I need to see you in private," Rick replied, taking the Professor's arm in one hand and opening the professor's own tent flap with the other, "Let's go in here, this won't take long."

"Sure, why not," said the Professor as he walked past Rick's arm. He walked over to his footlocker, opened it and took out a bottle of tequila. "Would you like a drink, Rick?"

"Yeah,ok, that sounds good, Doc," Rick

answered nonchalantly. Dr Comacho poured each of them a cupful, then sat down on his cot after handing Rick his drink.

"Sit down, amigo," the Professor said, gesturing towards the one canvas chair in the tent. He waited until Rick had gotten comfortable and then asked,"So, what is it that you want to discuss? All is going well, is it not?"

"Yeah, sure, Professor, you guys are doing a hell of a job here," Rick replied, smiling,"You know that and I know that." He paused and took a sip of tequila, wrinkling his face at it's strong bite, took a deep breath and said,"In fact, you guys have been doing too well, so well the investors aren't satisfied anymore with what you have been sending; they want more and they want it to come faster."

Dr Comacho jumped up and protested, "We've sent them some important finds, unique artifacts they aren't going to be able to get anywhere else!" Rick looked up resignedly at the Professor. He knew the man wouldn't take this too easily but he had to follow orders. The Professor and the others were ok people, but he had ambitions and would do whatever it took to get where he wanted to go. And Mr Bolina didn't like failure or excuses, just results. He said calmly to Dr Comacho, "I know, but now they want some larger pieces and more of the jade."

"The jade!" exclaimed Dr Comacho," the jade is to be the centerpiece of my exhibit!" He started pacing up and down the small tent, smacking his fist into his other hand, then looked cynically at Rick and said, "For some reason people seem to be attracted to great wealth, and the 'priceless' jade necklace would get the people into the museum where they might get an education in spite of themselves." The Professor stopped in front of Rick and looked wildly down at him. "They can't have the jade," he said vehemently, "And what do you mean, larger pieces? We can't get anything out unless it will fit in a suitcase!"

"Whoa,calm down now, Professor," Rick said soothingly as he stood up and walked over to the cot, "Sit down here and I'll explain it to you." He went back to the canvas chair and said, "The guys are getting tired of the suitcase route, so they want to bring their own plane in here, load it up, and adios!"

"Their own plane," the Professor interjected," they'll never get clearance, how are they going to do it?"

"You let us worry about that, ok Doc?" replied Rick, "You just get this stuff together." He handed Dr Comacho a list of the investor's "desires".

"No," said the Professor after a quick glance at the list, jumping up and towering over the seated Archetti, "I won't do it. It's too dangerous. The plane is bound to arouse suspicion, and if we get found out I'll be ruined and the whole project could be stopped." Rick stood straight up, forcing Dr Comacho to take a half step back, stared him coldly in the eye and said,   "That's right, if you get exposed for the liar and schemer that you are, you would be in disgrace, and so would your daughter, and probably the whole expedition would die on the vine." Rick smiled sarcastically as he said, "As I see it, you have a fifty-fifty chance with the plane, or . . ." He let his voice trail off as he looked steadily, emotionlessly into the Professor's eyes. The Professor had turned pale at Rick's words and now he just looked away and sat back down on the bunk, with the same stare of blank desperation as a mouse being toyed with by a cat. He looked disconsolately at the list in his hand and said to Archetti in a subdued voice,

"Give us some time to get this organized, okay Rick?"

"The jade too?" Rick asked, looking down at the Professor. Dr Comacho looked up sadly from his humped over position on the bunk,

"Yes, yes, everything, anything you guys need we will get it"

"Okay, Doc," replied Rick, grinning as he walked over and opened the tent flap, "No rush, take all the time you need, just keep me posted." "Don't worry, Professor," he said as he turned to walk out, "I think you made the right decision." With that he walked out into the clear night, leaving the Professor with his tequila and his broken pride.

*   *   *

The next day Dr Comacho stayed in his tent all day, except for a trip in the afternoon to Miguel's warehouse with the investor's 'wish list'. That evening he gathered Elena, Mitch, Teo, and Louis in his tent. It was a beautiful evening, one of those magnificent nights that only happen out in the wilderness, when the air is achingly clear and the blanket of brilliant stars filling the sky seems to come down to almost rub against the tree tops, when people outside just automatically speak in low, hushed tones. It was a clear night, but still, with practically no breeze, and what was really blanketing the jungle atmosphere was the oppressive humidity, not the cool looking swath of stars overhead, and the little group of archeologists and adventurers was suffering along with all the warm-blooded creatures of the sub-tropical jungle. All three guys had bottles of lukewarm beer in their hands as they shifted around trying to make themselves comfortable between the chair, the cot, and the footlocker. After they had all settled down the Professor started, "Since we are all in this together, and because you have been giving me such strong support, I feel it is only fair to keep you informed of what is happening."

"Uh oh, this doesn't sound too good," Mitch said cynically, "What is Mr Archetti up to now?" "Oh, Mitch, don't be so negative," replied Elena, her voice turning serious as she asked her father, "What is it ,Papa? What do they want from us now?" The Professor stood up and started pacing up and down the narrow space in the tent. He looked at them each in turn, his daughter and his three gringo friends, and said,

"Well, I'm being pressured to send more, larger objects, and . . .more of the jade."

"No, no," exclaimed Elena, jumping up and grabbing her father's arm, "Tat is all necessary for the exhibit, we can't let that go!" Teo and Louis just sat shaking their heads as Elena asked imploringly, "You told him no, didn't you ,Papa? You told him they couldn't just have anything they want, didn't you?" Dr Comacho stood still as he said in a

low voice,   "Mr
Archetti threatened to expose me, to leak word
of our dealings to the academic community,
perhaps even the authorities." The doctor sat
slowly back down as he looked around the tent,
trying not to look into anybody's eyes. "Either
way we're through," he said sadly.

"Hey," exclaimed Mitch, jumping up and
clenching his fists," somebody ought to do
something about Mr Rick Archetti, and I
volunteer!"

"Yeah, I wouldn't mind a shot or two at
him either," said Louis, throwing a vicious left
hook, right cross combination at his shadow on
the wall of the tent.

"Wait a minute, calm down boys," the
Professor said quietly, "It's not Archetti
anyway, he's just a messenger boy, not the
boss." The guys reluctantly settled down, with
some grumbling and fists smacking into palms,
as Elena asked, feeling sick to her stomach over
her father's capitulation, "All right, since we are
forced to cooperate, what are we going to do?
We can't send anything out on the plane that
won't fit into a suitcase, can we?" she said

resignedly. As an answer to that the Professor pulled the 'wish list' out of his pocket and handed it to Elena, with Teo looking over her shoulder. Elena gasped and Teo slowly sucked in his breath as they looked at the demands of the investors. The lintels over doorways, friezes from facia stone, jade from the burial chambers and more, sacred objects, large objects, some of everything. Elena looked up with tears in her large, Indian-black eyes and half whispered just one word,

"How?" The Professor stood in front of her and took her hands in his, looked deeply into her eyes, and said,

"Don't worry, daughter, everything is going to be all right . . ." He shifted awkwardly, glanced quickly around the tent and said, "I love you, and I won't let anything happen to you."   "Yeah, and us too," said Mitch as Teo and Louis nodded and patted her on the back. Mitch turned back to Dr Comacho, "Sure, but how? What's the plan?"

"They are bringing their own plane in," the Professor stated in a matter of fact way, "So what we have to do is gather the load down at Miguel's"

"An airplane!" exclaimed Elena, all excited again, "Isn't that awfully risky? What about clearance? What about customs, the manifest . . .?" The professor cut her off by raising his hand in front of her,

"Yes, it is risky, but we have no choice," he said resignedly. "Besides," he said earnestly, taking Elena's hand again and looking at Mitch, Teo, and Louis each in turn, "This is the last one, the last time we will have to do this." He silenced their questions with a raised finger and said, "The only concession I demanded was to be paid up front, in cash and in full. With that money we will have enough to take an exhibit on the road, a small but important exhibit." He looked around at their gloomy expressions, "Don't you get it? With the interest generated by our exhibit we should finally be able to raise enough funds to continue our work without Mt Archetti and his bosses. That's what we want, right?"

"Right, Professor," Mitch said as he stood and walked over to Dr Comacho and extended his hand, which Dr Comacho took in a firm handshake. "We are behind you all the way, Doc," he said, "We'll get through this together." There really wasn't much more to say, so they talked a little while about the mundane details of everyday life on the dig, and then slowly separated, each going to his own place with his own thoughts.

"So, what do you think of this deal?" Mitch asked Teo and Louis as they worked the next day.

"It stinks," said Louis disgustedly, "Those guys want it all . . . I'm tired of working for them!" He stopped and the anger went out of his voice as he said, "Yeah, but there isn't much we can do about it." Teo straightened up from where he was nailing a crate together around a lintel, took the nails out of his mouth and said,

"But what about the Professor's plan? Once we have enough money we will be free of those gangsters forever."

"Oh, come on, Teo," Mitch retorted, "Do you really believe that Rick and his bosses will let Dr Comacho off the hook? Once those kind of people get their claws into you they bleed you dry."

"Yeah, I think Mitch is right, Teo," Louis put in," it's not just the money they are holding over him now, it's the threat of exposure, it's extortion. These people don't give a damn about Dr Comacho's reputation or what happens to us or the heritage of a whole nation. They want everything and will do just about anything to get it."

"Yes, that's true," Teo came back, "But the one thing these 'private investors' can't take is the glare of public scrutiny. Once the Professor's exhibit gets going they won't be able to say anything, after all, they're involved in this too."

"Yeah, and we're involved," Mitch said, jabbing his finger at each of them and then himself, "You, you, and me. I mean, poaching monkeys or selling the jaguar skin on the black market was one thing, but this deal is heavy, big-time serious. We are foreigners here and we could definitely all land in jail."

"Well, what should we do then," a

confused Louis asked his friend Mitch, who he had come to respect a lot in just the few months that they had known each other, especially after what they had been through already in just those few months, "We can't just leave, can we? I mean the Prof, Elena . . ."

"Oh, sure, they are counting on us," Mitch broke in cynically, "But this is a volunteer thing, you know, and I think we have done enough already, we could leave at any time and not feel bad."

"Come on, Mitch, you don't mean that," countered Teo vehemently, his voice rising with his agitation as he stepped over in front of Mitch and grabbed both his shoulders," you're telling us that you can just walk away from Elena right now when she needs you so much?"

"No, no, you're right, Teo," Mitch replied, looking at his friend and then lowering his head to look disconsolately at the ground, "It just hurts me to see her so wound up in this thing, and I'm not sure I want to have to watch this fiasco go down." Teo held onto Mitch's shoulders and waited for him to look up. He knew why his friend was worried, they all were, because Elena hadn't taken her father's news too well. The combination of anger, disappointment, doubt, and confusion was churning all around inside of her, creating a lot of stress, even though she bravely tried to go about her business as if nothing was wrong. When Mitch met his eyes again Teo said gently,

"I know how much of a drag it is to see Elena so upset, but us bailing out on them now is certainly not going to help, and besides, you know that everyone in this thing really wants it to work, so I'm sure that it will come off okay, right amigo?"

"Well, I hope you are right, Teo," replied Mitch, "But I still don't like this 'Midnight Artifact Supply' deal we have got going here. I remember from my scamming days that anything that can go wrong, probably will go wrong, and I always liked a little back-up going for me." Louis put down his saw and came over to where Mitch was stacking wood for crating.

"What did you have in mind?" he asked conspiratorially, waving Teo over. The three guys put their heads together for a few minutes and then stepped back, with Louis nodding and

Teo shaking his head.

"Tomorrow we will talk to Herman and Perez and get this thing set up," Mitch said confidently, "now let's get back to work."

Chapter Eleven: Double Cross

Mitch stood uneasily by the side of the airstrip in the strange hush that seems to come over wild country in the last moments of twilight. The frogs, crickets, and night birds were just beginning their evening song, the mosquitoes buzzing out in force as the active creatures of the day gave way to the active creatures of the night, a thin line of egrets straggling across the last of the red sky on their way to roost. Mitch was again struck by their isolation out here, how far they were from anything. "Oh, well," he thought, "This is what I wanted I guess, an adventure." The only thing that broke up the natural air of the evening was the sharp odor of aviation fuel, three drums of which were sitting next to the little shack. Alongside of them were the artifacts, neatly crated and stacked in rows next to the runway. Two weeks after the group's discussion in Dr Comaco's tent, Rick Archetti had returned, gone down to Miguel's with the Professor and finalized his bosses' choices from the list. He said that the investors had agreed to the Professor's stipulation of cash payment, that he would be on the plane and would deliver it himself. He also gave them a date and a short system of light signals, mainly to tell the plane not to land if things weren't okay on the ground. But there wasn't much that could go wrong because a man of Dr Comacho's stature could do what he wanted in such a small village and the local authorities didn't question his activities at all. So, all that remained for the guys to do was to go to Miguel's, where the artifacts had been stored, pick up the chosen ones and truck them out to the airstrip. Now they were standing in the dense darkness of early night, just before the billions of stars that crowded the clear jungle nights were to come out, with Dr Comacho and Elena, Mitch and Teo between the fuel drums and the artifacts, Louis and Herman behind them in the bush, and Perez farther down the runway, near where the plane would turn around. The guys were armed with the old guns that Herman and Perez had managed to scrounge up after Mitch had talked to them. In addition to their old faithful twenty-two rifle from the jaguar hunt, they had come up with a pair of old birding guns, one a single barreled .410 shotgun, but the other a pretty serious twelve gauge double- barreled shotgun. The team of Louis and Herman had the rifle and the .410, with Perez holding the heaviest piece at the end of the runway, Mitch figuring that he would have the best chance of stopping the airplane if they needed to. An obviously tense and worried Dr Comacho went over to where Elena and Teo were matching the crates to the inventory she was holding, put his arm around her and said, somewhat unconvincingly,

"Don't worry, Elena, everything is going to turn out all right." She turned and took his hands in hers and said resignedly,

"Yes, father, I'm sure it will." She looked around sadly and said, "I just hate to see these things go, they are all so irreplaceable."

"Yes, but you forget," came back Dr Comacho, "These things represent our freedom from Mr Archetti and his bosses, they represent our future, our legacy really."

"Well, I hope you are right about that," she replied, "But what about the guys, is it really necessary for them to be eaten alive in the brush?"

"That was my idea," put in Mitch, "There is a lot of money involved and we are pretty far out in the bushes here, and I would rather be safe than sorry, so just indulge me, all right?" Elena took a step over and stood next to

Mitch,

"You just don't like Rick much, right?" when Mitch started to protest she cut him off with, "I know Rick and his bosses are greedy people, but do you really think they are dangerous?" Before Mitch could reply the Professor silenced them both with a finger to his lips and then to his ear,

"I hear them," he said, "Get the flashlights ready, they're coming!"

Sounding at first like a large mosquito flying close to the ear, the noise of the plane's engines grew louder and louder until Mitch, standing at the front of the little group, spotted it and pointed it out as it described a gentle curving bank around the far end of the runway. The bare whiteness of the coral airstrip stood out in the soft, liquid light of the now rising moon, in stark contrast to the dense, dark jungle surrounding it. As prearranged the pilot would need no lights on the strip, but the Professor and Mitch both trained their flashlights on the windsock, the plane having to both land and take-off into the wind. Each member of the little expedition stood nervously with his or her own thoughts as they watched the plane circle the runway once and then come in, a little puff of blue smoke coming off the tires when the wheels first touched the rough coral surface, the propeller's pitch deepening as the tires screeched again and again as the pilot stood on the brakes to get the airplane stopped in time. Mitch was surprised again by how loud the engines seemed when the pilot revved them up one at a time to get the plane turned around and taxi-ing toward the shed. He looked around anxiously and then laughed to himself as he thought, "What am I worried about? There's no one around to hear anything, maybe I am getting too paranoid." He shrugged but it didn't make him feel any better as he watched the plane roll to a halt near where they were standing and the door open to let out Mr Rick Archetti, carrying a brown briefcase chained to his left wrist, and a large, tough-looking guy who Mitch had never seen before, carrying what looked like a military issue sub-machine gun.

"Ah, Dr Comacho," Rick half yelled over

the noise of the still idling engines, "How are you, my friend?" He strode quickly over to where the Professor was standing by the fuel drums, took the Professor's outstretched hand and shook it exuberantly. After accepting Dr Comacho's mumbled greeting and with a quick nod to Elena, Mitch and Teo, Archetti said, "Well, I see you have everything together here, that's good, but where are the other guys?" He looked around suspiciously at the shed and the nearest trees at the edge of the field, "You know, to help us load?" Elena looked at the guy with the machine gun and started to say something but the Professor cut her off and said with a smile,

"We just wanted to keep it to a minimum, you understand I'm sure. But don't worry, we will get the job done." As he pulled the inventory sheet out of his pocket he asked, "You do have the money, don't you?" Archetti laughed and turned to the fuel drums. He placed the briefcase on top of one and started turning the dials of the combination lock.

"Of course I have the money," he said as he raised the lid to reveal the tightly wrapped packages of bills stacked closely in the briefcase, "I trust you, you trust me, we trust each other, right?" He looked over the handsome leather case full of money and gave Dr Comacho his best good buddy smile as he finished talking.

"Oh, is that so," Elena broke in archly, "If that is true then what is he here for?" she asked as she looked pointedly at Archetti's guard. Archetti snapped the lid back down on the briefcase and then turned to Elena, smiling with his arms spread out in a conciliatory gesture as he said,

"Hey, we are a long way from anywhere and this is a lot of money, that's all. And it wasn't my idea, the investors insisted." He took the list from Dr Comacho, and as he looked it over he said, "Okay, Billy, we're among friends, put that thing down and make yourself useful, help us load this stuff, ok?" The big guy just nodded and leaned the machine gun against the nearest drum. He then walked over to the largest crate and grabbed one end, bending over to get a good grip and looking at Mitch and Teo standing to the side. Teo immediately jumped over to grab the other end and Mitch breathed a sigh of relief as he said,

"Ok, let's get this bird loaded." They worked purposely for about a half an hour, with Archetti and Dr Comacho standing by the door of the plane, checking each object off the list as it was loaded, Mitch and Archetti's man Billy teaming up on the larger oblects, and Teo and Elena carrying whatever they could. The pilot came back from the cockpit to supervise the loading because the weight distribution could be crucial to the plane getting off the ground in the short distance available on the little runway. It was hot, hard work in the cramped and close cargo hold of the plane but the physical activity felt good as a release for all the tension they had been feeling while waiting. They all started to relax and even joke a little as they worked and Mitch wondered what the guys that were getting eaten up by insects in the brush would have to say to him later, when the deal was done. "Oh, well," he thought, beginning to feel a little foolish about his worries, "Maybe I am getting too old for this stuff." He and Archetti's man held the last crate in place as Teo and the pilot strapped it down. Archetti, Elena, and Dr Comacho had already stepped over to the fuel drums and as the guys left the plane Rick waved them over to where they were using the drums as an impromptu desk.

"Come on, you guys," he said, placing the briefcase on top of the fuel canister again, "You'll want to see this, this is what it's all about." Mitch went over and stood next to Elena, putting his arm around her protectively, while Teo went over next to the Professor. Archetti's guard Billy strolled over and picked up his weapon, and hung back by the plane. Archetti shook the Professor's hand again and smiled at each of them in turn, and said, "Good job, Dr Comacho, it's a pleasure working with you." He glanced around again at everyone's position. "And now, the key to get this damned chain off of my wrist," he said as he reached inside his coat. But instead of a key he came out with a pistol, aimed point-blank at the Professor's chest and fired twice. Time seemed to slow down, almost freeze for Mitch as he saw the weapon come out. He felt himself start to move, grabbing Elena's shoulders as if in a trance, fascinated by the pistol and its progress from the coat to fully extended in Archetti's hand. He could hear loudly and clearly the click of the mechanism as the hammer of the revolver locked into place. The sound of the first shot was like an explosion going off in his head, but it snapped him out of his trance as its echoes and the echoes of the second shot reverberated over the contrasting silence of the frightened jungle. He pulled Elena with him as he dove to the side behind the fuel drums. He saw the Professor falling wildly backwards, taking a stunned Teo down as Teo tried to catch him beneath the arms, the Professor's blood pumping out over Teo's hands and forearms. Mitch's mind was racing but it wasn't coming up with any good ideas as he saw Archetti wave Billy towards where Mitch was covering Elena behind the drums, then point his revolver at Teo, who was half sitting, half lying on the ground trying to hold Dr Comacho's head up. He heard Archetti say, "You waste the hippie, and I'll . . ." But that was as far as he got as suddenly from the jungle came the blast of the old shotgun and the sharp crack of the twenty-two. Mitch saw Billy, crouching forward with the machine gun ready to tear them apart, catch the full load of the .410 in the throat and lower face. He grunted out a strangled scream as the impact drove him staggering back towards the plane. His left hand flew to his torn face and his mangled throat as his right hand tightened on the trigger of the machinegun, ripping off a burst that threw dirt on Mitch as the bullets just missed the line of drums. He lurched back, crashing into the fuselage of the plane before pitching forward on the machinegun to gurgle out his last breath. All this took place in less time than it took for the first echoes of the shotgun blast to bounce back off the dense trees surrounding the airstrip.

At the same moment that Billy met his end, Archetti was hit by the twenty-two fired by Louis. His mind filled for an instant with fear and pain as the bullet stabbed through the muscle of his shoulder and punched into the bone, causing him to drop the revolver in front of Teo. But his faculties came back to him quickly and he reacted with anger, cursing

Mitch and shaking his fist towards the fuel drums.

"You son-of-a-bitch, you mother-fucking goddamn hippie, I'm gonna get your fucking ass!" Teo was watching in stunned fascination, but now started to struggle out from under Dr Comacho and move toward the gun lying on the ground. Archetti saw him and started to bend down to pick up the pistol when his mind was changed by the angry sound of a twenty-two round buzzing by his head. He realized that if he hadn't bent down it would have gotten him so he decided to bug out. He turned, still in a crouch, and ran towards the plane, crashing down on all fours in a cloud of dust as the pattern of pellets from the .410 caught him in the left leg. He yelled at the pilot as he scuttled towards the open door of the already running airplane. "Go, let's go!" he shouted, crawling in, "Let's get the fuck out of here!" Archetti's left leg was still hanging out as the pilot gunned the engines, holding the brakes on one wheel to whip the plane around in a 180 degree turn to start taxi-ing up the runway. As the plane was turning the blast of air from the propwash enveloped the tragic scene by the fuel drums in dust and wind-whipped leaves. Shielding their eyes with their hands, Mitch and Elena jumped up and ran to where Teo, who had struggled out from under the Professor, knelt next to his friends bleeding body, still holding his head up off the ground. Elena jumped down next to her father, cradling his upper body in her arms, shielding his face from the propwash with her shoulder. "Papa, Papa," she cried, rocking back and forth sobbing, her face a grotesque mask of pain and sorrow, her bloodshot, red and swollen eyes pouring out tears which made dark streaks down her dust-caked cheeks. "He's going to be all right, isn't he?" she pleaded to Teo, who just nodded and squeezed her arm, still too stunned to say anything. Mitch looked up in time to see Louis and Herman running towards them from the brush.

"Let's get that bastard !" he yelled, his confused mind racing, bending down to scoop up the pistol that Archetti had dropped, and then running up the airstrip after the retreating plane. He waved for Herman and Louis to join him, snapping off a couple of shots at the now fish-tailing plane, more in anger and frustration than in any hope of stopping it. The guys turned and started running across the low grass of the airstrip's edge at an angle that would bring them even with Mitch, Louis pausing once to fire the even more hopeless twenty-two at the plane's tires, the whining screech of the ricochet proving his miss. Herman was holding his fire for a shot more within the little shotgun's range, but he was yelling his head off as he ran down the coral.

"Cuidado, cuidado amigo, watch out!" he shouted to Perez as he and Mitch and Louis saw him come scuttling out of the bush under the cover of the propwash as the plane reached the end of the runway, did another 180, and started to pull away from him on it's take-off roll. The guys stopped and crouched next to the coral strip, getting ready to hit the plane with everything they had as it went by. But Mitch was distracted by Elena's voice yelling, "No, Mitch, no!" over and over. He turned to see Elena running up the strip yelling and waving her arms. She was running because at the sound of Mitch's and Louis's shots the Professor had regained consciousness in Elena's arms. He sat bolt upright with surprising strength, looked down the runway and then sagged back against Teo and Elena, a look like a bad memory on his face. He turned his head to look up at Elena and started mumbling,

"The artifacts, the artifacts, my daughter, I'm so sorry," he shook his head and mumbled incoherently, then suddenly looked straight into her eyes, "The artifacts are . . . . they are . . ." But he could go no farther and sank back into unconsciousness in his sitting position on the ground between them. Elena struggled to her feet, passing Dr Comacho's weight to Teo as she rose,

"Hold him, Teo," she sobbed, and then to Dr Comacho, "Don't worry, Papa, I understand, the artifacts are too valuable to be destroyed no matter what happens. I'll save them, I'll stop the guys!" Now she was bounding down the runway towards Mitch, with tears streaming down her face and the front of her shirt covered with blood, trying to hold back her sobbing and gasping for breath long enough to shout at the guys not to shoot. She shrieked hysterically and nearly fell when she saw the flash and heard the boom of the ancient twelve-gauge as Perez let go a blast at the tail of the plane from his crouch at the end of the runway. It didn't slow the aircraft down at all but it did bring Mr Rick Archetti to the cargo door with another gun in his hand. He leaned out as the plane was gathering speed and took a couple of blind shots behind him, where he had heard the shotgun, but then turned and saw a scene that caused him to smile wickedly as he braced himself in the doorway and steadied his grip for a better shot. The guys had gotten Elena's message, and now Louis and Herman crouched indecisively in the tall grass as Mitch jumped up and started running back to Elena. Teo had also reacted to the shotgun blast and Archetti's shots and was running as hard as he could after Elena, after having laid the still unconscious Professor gently down in a pool of his own blood. "Got to help the living," Mitch thought grimly as he pounded down the unforgiving coral, rapidly converging on Elena but also being caught by the now speeding plane. He looked back and saw Archetti crouched in the doorway, drawing a bead on the middle of his back. He leaped to the side just in time to hear the whine of the bullet rip past him and kick up an angry swarm of coral chips as it bounced off the runway and out into the jungle. Mitch felt the sting as the bits of rock caught him along his entire left side as he flew through the air in his desperate leap to avoid Archetti's shot. Just before he crashed painfully down into the rocks and sticks along the jungle clearing he saw Teo catch Elena and pull her down into the high grass, shielding her with his body, as Archetti laughed maniacally while speeding by, emptying the pistol into the brush at them as he went. Mitch dragged himself up, hardly feeling anything because of the adrenalin flowing through him, and ran to Teo and Elena, getting there in time to join Herman and Louis and Perez, who had run up the strip, chasing the speeding plane in futile anger and frustration. They watched with bitter resignation as the pilot gathered speed for lift-off, using all the distance he could because of the heavy load. They could still faintly hear

Archetti laughing and yelling but they couldn't tell what he was saying when they were all frozen into shock by the brilliant muzzle flash and roaring rip of the machine gun going through an entire clip. Dr Comacho had crawled over and gotten Billy's weapon, and now was up on one elbow, too weak to sit up but steadying the gun with one hand while squeezing the trigger with the other, raking the plane just as its wheels left the ground. There was a terrible shriek of metal tearing and glass shattering as the bullets tore through the plane down its entire length. The right engine coughed and choked into silence, thick black smoke and flames pouring out of it as the plane lurched crazily to the right, bouncing off it's landing gear and wing tip, whipped rapidly back to the left, nosed over and struck full force into the thick jungle at the end of the strip. The wings and engines on both sides were ripped off and the tail was sticking up almost vertically over the ruined cockpit where the pilot had died. The destroyed machine sat at deceptive rest for a few moments, hissing and quietly dripping out its vital fluids, then suddenly roared into flames as the fuel from the ruptured tanks poured onto the hot engine parts. The flames snapped the little group out of their state of shock and they all started running toward the weird, brilliant pool of light provided by the towering flames of the ruined plane. Just before the burning wreck exploded completely, they saw a body roll out of the cargo door and crash to the ground. It was Archetti, terribly burned and battered, but still holding the pistol in one hand and still with the briefcase chained to his wrist. The guys and Elena were just reaching the Professor as they heard Archetti scream a howling curse at them as he waved the gun over his head before crashing off into the bush. Elena again jumped down next to her father where he had slumped forward off his elbow onto the machine gun. Gently she put her arm around his shoulders, pulling him over onto her lap, cradling his head in the crook of her elbow. Tears streamed down her face as she sobbed over and over,

"No, Papa, why, Papa, what . . . why, Papa, why? "The blood from her myriad of cuts and scrapes from the coral mingled with her father's blood as the life flowed out of him. The guys all gathered around them, Teo and Louis trying to comfort Elena, Perez and Herman hanging back nervously scanning the jungle where Archetti had disappeared, while Mitch knelt down in front of the Professor to try to help him. But as Mitch was trying to unbutton the Professor's blood-soaked shirt, the Professor revived, suddenly clear in his mind and calm, eerily calm, as he reached out his hand to stop Mitch. "Ah, Mitch," he said, his hand resting lightly on Mitch's forearm, "Mitch, my good gringo friend, I knew you would be here, but don't bother, amigo, I'm dying, I know it."

"No, no, Papa," Elena moaned desperately, "You are going to be all right. We are going to take care of you. You are not going to die over any silly old relics." Elena sobbed emphatically as she rocked the Professor gently in her arms, her head on his shoulder.

"She's right, Doc," Mitch said easily as he started to open the shirt again, "Don't try to talk, just rest, we'll take care of you."

"No, no," whispered the Professor as he

raised his finger for silence one last time, "Let me talk while I still can, the relics," he turned his head to look up into Elena's anguished eyes, "Elena, my daughter, those artifacts were fakes, copies . . ." His eyes half closed and his voice trailed off as his head sank toward his shattered chest, "Miguel, Miguel, see Miguel," he mumbled, "I couldn't, I could not part with . . . Those people don't deserve . . . our people, rightfully." He sighed as his chin settled down to his sternum, then raised his head up suddenly, looked at Mitch through half closed eyes and said, "Mitch, my friend, you were right, those people . . . those people should never be trusted . . . I gambled and lost . . ." He tried a little choking chuckle as he said, "But we surprised them, didn't we, amigo?" He coughed and turned again to Elena, not hearing Mitch's sobbing,

"Yeah, sure Professor, sure." Mitch felt the tears pouring down his face as he stared over at Elena, a look that has come down through centuries of tragedy on her face as she looked down into her dying father's eyes. He said,

"Elena, my daughter, forgive me, I did what I thought I had to do . . . our dreams . . . our project . . . your mother." He was drifting in and out now, his voice getting lower and lower, down to an almost inaudible whisper as he said, "Mitch, take care of her." Mitch just nodded in stunned silence, his mind overloaded and overwhelmed. The Professor's voice got a little clearer as he said, "Elena, I love you . . . remember I . . ." He sighed his last as his head fell to his chest and his hand fell off Mitch's forearm. Elena let out a keening wail, a howl of agonized grief and protest.

"No, no," she shrieked, screaming out her sorrow and her anger over an unknowing, uncaring jungle. She then buried her face in her dead father's neck, sobbing violently and rocking back and forth on her knees. The guys again leaned in to comfort her, Mitch helplessly repeating her name over and over softly, when suddenly he stood up straight, pounded his fist into his palm and snarled,

"Archetti, you scumbag, I'm gonna kill you!" His voice kept rising until he was screaming out into the bush, "You bastard, I'm coming for you!" The reflection of the still burning plane in his eyes mirrored the rage he was feeling within as he told Teo and Louis, "You guys stay here and take care of Elena, I'll handle this." He opened the revolver he had and counted his shots. "Two rounds left, that ought to do it," he mumbled as he strode away toward the wrecked plane and where he had last seen Archetti. When Perez and Herman tried to fall in with him he just growled, "No, he's mine," and they understood, although they tried to get him to take the shotgun. He said, "No, this will do," holding up the revolver, "One shot is all I need for a snake. You guys keep those in case he circles back." With that he turned and started to jog, then run up the runway towards the plane's funeral pyre.

Chapter Twelve : Mitch and Rick

As Mitch reached the spot where Archetti had plunged into the brush, he was still in the grasp of a wild rage, so he crashed right in after him, but as he stopped to catch his breath just inside the edge of the jungle, he felt his crazy anger begin to ebb. Maybe it was the physical exertion of his all-out sprint down the airstrip, more likely it was the beginnings of battle fatigue in an unprepared adventurer who had gotten more than he bargained for. Whatever the reason Mitch felt his anger turning to apprehension as he crouched down in the brush, hiding in the dark from the hellish red-orange glow and dancing shadows produced by the fire. The memories of his terrible night in the jungle chasing Elena, of the ants and the horror of the feeling of hopelessness and despair as he felt himself going down came flooding back to him. The adrenalin was definitely gone from him now as he hesitated, remembering how difficult Elena had been to find in the dark jungle. The surreal light from the plane's fire didn't penetrate very far into the dense vegetation and although there were a few broken branches that he could see, he didn't think that they would help to find Archetti now. The aggressive insects of the tropical rain forest were starting to find Mitch and he was considering returning to the others to restart the search with help and in daylight when he heard it. At first he thought it was some kind of large animal, angry, perhaps another jaguar, disturbed by all the violence in his fiefdom and coming after them. But it was Archetti, calling out to him, cursing him and challenging him to come on.

"Hey, hippie," he wailed out in an ugly, horrible voice, "Come on you chicken-shit hippie, come get me if you've got the balls!" Mitch froze momentarily and then turned instinctively towards the voice as Archetti shrieked dementedly, "I've got the money and I've got the gun, and I'll have your ass before it's over!" He laughed maniacally as he called out, "Come on you sneaky bastard, I'm not very far away, come and get it." Mitch shifted the pistol from his right hand to his left, so he could wipe his sweaty palm on his shirt as he listened intently in the direction where he could hear Archetti moving through the brush. He didn't know if Archetti was moving toward him or away, but it didn't matter, for all of Mitch's fear and even most of his anger were gone now, replaced by a calm intensity, a grim determination to finish the job, to rid the world of this rotten bastard once and for all. He tightened his grip on the revolver as he started moving in a crouch, sometimes crawling on his knees and one hand, heading toward the sound of Archetti's tormented voice as he continued to curse Mitch, the Professor, and everyone else involved. For several minutes Mitch pushed and slid through the wet, tangled vegetation, trying to move mostly when Archetti was yelling, following him deeper and deeper into the jungle. Now Mitch moved ahead very cautiously, pausing often to peer uselessly into the blackness and to listen intently, trying to get a fix on the direction of the sounds of the wounded and dangerous man over the constant background of chirps, croaks, and calls of the billions of creatures of the tropical night. Now it appeared that Archetti had stopped. His angry curses and taunts, although weaker, were still coming constantly, and Mitch pinpointed the spot in his mind as being about thirty feet ahead and to the left. As Mitch moved to within fifteen feet of his adversary he dropped to his belly, crawling along slowly, parting the branches ahead of him with his left hand, his right firmly grasping the pistol at the ready. Mitch's hand was shaking and he was moving very slowly and carefully when he pushed aside a large frond and saw Archetti about eight feet away. Mitch was shocked by what he saw and he froze, the pistol in his right hand pointed directly at Archetti's chest. The former sharp dresser from Miami was half sitting, half lying in some dirt and low bushes, leaning back against a large banyan tree, the briefcase in his lap, his legs sprawled out to either side. His fancy safari jacket and designer jeans were torn and burned into unrecognizable tatters, exposing the blackened skin and angry red fissures of severely burned flesh down his entire left side. His right shoe was gone but a thin wisp of smoke rose horribly from the melted clump of his left one as his disfigured and half bald head alternated between resting on his scratched and bleeding chest and bobbing up to yell out his increasingly feeble curses at them all, but especially Mitch. Suddenly, with all the instincts of a cornered animal, Archetti stiffened. He held his head up and stared intently around him, to the edges of the little clearing bordered by the tree he was leaning against and spoke out in a clear, strong voice, "Where are you, you bastard, I know you're there somewhere." His head stopped scanning to gaze directly towards where Mitch was lying, "Come on you chicken-shit bastard, make your move!" Mitch's response was to pull back the hammer of the revolver, the sharp click as it locked into place resonating in the suddenly silent jungle as he stared down the barrel at Archetti's broken body. "Come on you fucking wimp," called out the near delirious Archetti, "Shoot me, you damn hippie! Come on, let's fight it out!" Mitch watched over the sights as Archetti struggled to lift the gun that was more or less lying on his right hand.

"Shoot him," Mitch thought angrily, "Shoot the bastard, end it now!" But he couldn't. His finger just didn't tighten on the trigger. "Come on," he spoke to himself under his breath, "Come on, kill the scumbag, you hate him, he killed your friend, he's evil, just kill him." He argued irrationally with himself as Archetti continued to try to raise the pistol, still staring toward Mitch, nothing but hatred in his one remaining eye. "You killed the jaguar," Mitch reasoned with himself, "And he was a far more noble creature than this scumbag. You killed the monkeys, too, and they were innocent." But this was a human, evil, yes, but hurt and helpless. And Archetti was right, he was a hippie. Deep down somewhere in him he had never let go of those basic hippie beliefs about peace, love, and the value of human life. About Karma, how it would come back to you, how you couldn't defeat evil with more evil. All the time these thoughts were racing through Mitch's mind, he was training the sights of the pistol on Archetti's forehead, watching

Archetti's wobbly arm making progress toward bringing the gun to a firing position. "Does he have any shots left in that thing?" wondered Mitch as he took a deep breath and tightened his finger on the trigger. His body stiffened as Archetti raised his right knee to stabilize the revolver, now pointed pretty much directly at Mitch. "Archetti, I hate your goddamn guts," he muttered under his breath, hating Archetti, hating the jungle, hating greedy people, hating the whole goddamn situation he found himself in, in the middle of a goddamn jungle. With his finger on the trigger, the sights of the gun on Archetti's forehead, just a thought away from blowing Archetti's brains all over the banyan tree, Mitch remained locked in this horrible, tragic tableau, surrounded and entrapped by the all-encircling jungle.

*   *   *

As the minutes crept by the little group

back at the shed was getting more and more uneasy. When Mitch ran down the coral strip and plunged into the jungle, things had been happening so quickly that none of them had any chance to think about the situation, they had been just reacting to it. But now as the leaping flames of the burning plane settled down to low, smoldering fires, nearly smothered by their own oily black smoke, rising in a thick column from the blackened, fire-made clearing in the soggy brush, darkness, silence, and anxiety washed over them. Teo and Louis had led Elena away from her father's side, pulling her to her feet and walking her over to the side of the shed after Teo had laid his jacket over the Professor's body. Teo noted grimly to himself that the Profesor's features in death showed none of the stress and concern that so marked his life, instead his face appeared calm, composed, as if he had accepted his fate and was satisfied with the results.

"A great man, a brave man," thought Teo, "He deserved better."

"Don't worry," he said softly to Elena as

he rejoined them, "He will be remembered, I promise you."

"I know," replied Elena wearily, taking his hand and looking up at him through still flowing eyes, her thin body racked by sobs as he put his arm around her to comfort her. Herman and Perez came up and offered their condolences, with Elena taking each one's hand in turn and thanking them for their help in everything. As Perez let go of her hand and stepped back into the little semi-circle around her, he asked, "Senorita Elena, what should we do now? Senor Mitch, should we go and try to find him? We heard Senor Archetti cursing before, but now nothing. Can we find him, or should we wait?" Elena took a deep breath and tried to stop sobbing as she looked around her at the troubled, expectant faces of her friends and co-workers.

"They are looking to me now," she thought and the thought gave her confidence. As she straightened up and wiped the tears off her cheeks with the back of her hand, she tried to think. The thick, low slung, brooding vegetation of the incredibly prolific tropical rain forest had swallowed all but the first of Archetti's angry cries and now the anquished group could hear nothing but the familiar sounds of the night time jungle beginning to return to full volume. "How long has it been," she wondered, "Five minutes? Ten minutes?" She assumed that Mitch had also heard the cries and was onto Archetti, tracking him somewhere in the brush. As her mind raced frantically through her alternatives, the shocking events of the last hours and weeks almost overwhelmed her. She sighed and took a tiny step back, burying her face in her hands, wanting nothing more than to slide down the shed wall behind her and dissolve into sorrow, to block out reality and just hide in her grief, but she didn't. Instead she turned to Louis to answer him when he pleaded,

"We've got to do something, we've got to help him somehow."

"Yeah, but what?" broke in Teo, "That jungle, at night . . ." Elena interrupted by raising one finger, then said,

"Well, first we'll move closer to where he went in, to listen and maybe call out to him, okay?" She looked around her at the guys nodding their approval, then started walking purposely up the runway, with just a single backward glance at the dark shape of her father's body lying near the fuel drums. The ragged little band of weary adventurers had almost reached what they guessed was the entry point of the deadly combatants, alternating between calling out to Mitch and listening intently for a reply when they were rooted to the spot by the booming report of a heavy caliber handgun. The echoes of the first shot had just about died down and they had started moving again when the second shot came, seeming even louder than the first. Elena raced frantically back and forth along the edge of the jungle near the skeleton of the dead airplane as the guys frantically renewed their calls to Mitch. Teo and Louis started to charge into the brush, but Elena, remembering her terrible night in the jungle and how easy it was to get lost, stopped them. "It's no use," she cried, "You'll never find him, you'll probably get lost too!"

"Goddamn it, we have to do

something," cursed Louis, brandishing the twenty-two rifle angrily.

"The best thing we can do now," argued Elena forcefully, "Is to stay here and give him a direction with our voices." With that she stood in one spot and started calling out, "This way, Mitch, follow my voice, right over here!" Teo and Herman and Perez joined her, with Louis muttering,

"Which 'him' are we going to get?" as he checked the twenty-two and dropped to one knee in the low brush.

*   *   *

Mitch stared at Archetti like a bird fascinated by a snake. He lay stock-still in the thick underbrush, ignoring the insects, ignoring his own sweat starting to run down his face. The only parts of his body moving were his fingers squirming on the grip of the revolver and his eyes, flicking from looking down the sights at Archetti's forehead to the gun in Archetti's hand. For now the dying gunman had managed to steady the pistol on his knee, forsaking for the moment his angry cursing to concentrate on pulling back the hammer of the pistol. Mitch's breath was coming in short gasps as he checked his dead aim on Archetti's forehead. He used his left hand to steady the base of the gun in his right hand and there was no way he could miss from where he was. But he just couldn't squeeze the trigger. To shoot even a deserving gangster would be to kill the ideals Mitch believed in and tried to live by. But he hated Archetti, hated what Archetti had done...could feel the hatred in him, and he couldn't deny it. "But that still doesn't make it right," Mitch thought, the thought coming from the part of his psyche where his ideals were desperately hanging on. But suddenly that and all other considerations were swept from Mitch's mind by the sound of Archetti's revolver hammer clicking into place and his maniacal laugh as he called out,

"I've got you now, you limp-dicked hippie bastard!" Mitch could see Archetti's hand tightening on the trigger and he could feel the evil hatred emanating from the pain in his adversary's broken body, from his shattered pride, as he called out, "Die, you son-of-a-bitch, die!" At the same moment that the hammer of Archetti's pistol came down, Mitch rolled to the side and fired, the booming blast of the handgun silencing all other noises of the jungle as the bullet ripped a six inch gouge out of the banyan tree a few inches above Archetti's head. All other noises except the metallic click of the hammer of Archetti's pistol striking the spent cartridge in the chamber of the empty gun. As Mitch rolled and fired he jumped to a crouch and crashed forward a couple of strides into the clearing, yelling out a spontaneous war cry and pulling the hammer back on his final round as he did so. Now he stood over his enemy, his gun pointed at the side of the Miami dude's head. Archetti made no move to raise the gun, now hanging heavily in his hand, getting lower and lower as his knee sagged down to the side. Instead he looked up at Mitch and smiled, a horrible, twisted smile on what was left of his face as he hissed at Mitch,

"I knew you couldn't do it, you wimp...you don't have the balls," he gasped out, his breath coming in short, erratic bursts, "No hippie bastard and a bunch of foreign hicks can get me . . . I'm Rick Archetti, from Miami . . . I'm smart, I'm tough . .. I'm . . . I'm . . ." With that he sort of settled to the right, the weight of the gun pulling his leg to the ground, his one remaining eye going wide and staring blankly into hell as he sighed out his last breath. Mitch stood over his finally stilled adversary and shook his head. He could feel the waves of anger and hatred washing up and down his body but mostly he just felt an immense relief. It was over, at last. Mitch had heard that dead people, especially enemies, always looked smaller after death, more vulnerable, weaker, like you couldn't believe they could have been so formidable.

"This is not the case with Mr Rick Archetti," thought Mitch as he stepped across him to reach the briefcase. He looked the same to Mitch, like he didn't belong there, his burned designer jeans and smart safari jacket looking even more out of place in death than in life. "Oh, well," Mitch thought as he put the barrel of the gun up against the wrist chain of the briefcase, "On with the living." The briefcase was charred a little on the outside but appeared to be intact. "You were right, Mr Rick Archetti, I couldn't do it," Mitch steadied his aim and squeezed off his last shot to cut the chain, "But I will take this." He squatted down next to the ruined body and picked up the briefcase. He stayed down at almost face level to the corpse, staring at it. He wanted to say something cool, something macho, but there really wasn't anything to say, so he just shook his head and stood up in the darkness. He turned toward where he could now hear the faint voices of his friends calling to him, clasped the briefcase to his chest and started pushing straight through the brush toward them, calling out as he went, "Don't shoot, Herman, Perez, Louis, it's me, I'm coming out." The jungle was as unforgiving as ever, slashing at him, scratching his hands and face, trying to confuse him with it's labyrinth of turns and thickets, but he ignored everything and kept on towards the ever louder voices of his friends. Finally he came crashing out of the grasp of the tropical vegetation into the clearing of the airstrip about thirty yards from his comrades. He tried to smile and hold up the briefcase as they ran to him but dissolved into tears along with everyone else as they hugged each other in a sobbing knot of humanity on the edge of the jungle airstrip under the billions and billions of stars of the tropical night.

Chapter Thirteen: Gringo Trail

Mitch stood awkwardly with Elena in the small lobby of the Hotel Astoria, his backpack leaning up against the wall with the rest of his gear. He thought Elena looked especially beautiful in her city clothes, a dark skirt and jacket outfit over a white blouse with ruffles on the cuffs and collar. The black ribbon around her neck and the briefcase in her hand made her look every inch the modern, aggressive but feminine business woman. But

Elena wasn't feeling very business-like now as she stepped close to Mitch, looked up at him with just a hint of tears in her eyes and said,

"Are you sure you want to go? I mean I could . . ." But Mitch stopped her by gently putting his finger to her lips. He put his hands on her shoulders, her hands resting lightly on his chest, and looked into her eyes.

"Come on, Elena," he said softly, "We went over this before, right?" He looked down at the nearly healed scratches on the back of Elena's hand. Although the action was all over when Mitch stumbled out of the jungle at the edge of the airstrip, the rest of the night and the next day were still an ordeal for the weary participants in the night's violent drama. After several moments of hugging and sobbing the little group almost automatically drifted back to the shed. They gathered next to the wall on the opposite side from the bodies of Dr Comacho and the gunman, Billy. They made their plans, which consisted mostly of sending off the ever dependable Herman and Perez in the truck to alert the local authorities, while Elena, Mitch, Louis, and Teo rested against the shed wall.

They waited in a kind of exhausted silence,
staring numbly at each other or down the strip,
their weary minds washed over by the
magnitude of the stunning events of the last
few hours. It didn't take long for Herman and
Perez to return with the local police, but the
locals didn't do much but give out very
welcome coffee and blankets to the tired
survivors, preferring to wait for morning and
the arrival of the top authorities that they had
radioed in from the capital. They did walk
around, probing the darkness with their
flashlights, checking out the wrecked plane and
shaking their heads as they talked among
themselves about 'crazy gringos'. One of them
approached Mitch and asked about the
briefcase, but he didn't push it when Mitch just
gripped it tighter and shook his head no. The
first authorities arrived about an hour after
dawn in a small plane, carrying the chief
inspector of police for the province and a
representative of the Bureau of Antiquities,
followed a while later by a helicopter with a
crash site team of medics and police. It took a
couple of hours all together for them to inspect

the site, photograph the positions of the bodies and even to find Archetti's body, inspect the wrecked plane and rope it off, and question everybody involved. Mitch was impressed by the courtesy and efficiency of the police but he was still worried about Elena. After they had rested while waiting for Herman and Perez to return, she appeared to rally when the top authorities arrived, speaking calmly when questioned. She told her story under perfect control, only starting to choke up when she got near the part where her father was shot. Although her lips quivered and tears came to her eyes she kept a grip on herself and finished with the inspector's questions. She calmly agreed with Mitch to turn the briefcase over to the authorities and let them decide what to do with it, then politely asked to be allowed to rest. She was being led away by a sympathetic officer when all her self control was shattered by the sight of her father's body with the others, lying in the terrible anonymous equality of the plastic bodybag. She screamed wildly in a fit of hysterical anger and tried to reach the row of bodies to pull her father away from the others, but she was held back by police and then sedated by a medic. It was terrible for Mitch to see her like that but he was relieved that she would get some respite from her anguish as he watched her consciousness give up the struggle and her body relax as she slid into a pattern of deep, slow breathing. Mitch was also glad to see her put into the airplane for the trip to the hospital in the capital instead of in the helicopter with the bodies. Mitch and the guys had to ride in the helicopter but were too tired to care. They were so tired in fact that after a few minutes of staring at the seemingly endless green carpet below them, they actually fell asleep, Mitch had to stretch his legs between two of the bags to get enough room.

They spent the first couple of weeks in the capital put up in the university dormitories, under a form of house arrest. They were not really under arrest though, since no one had been charged with any crime pending the outcome of the investigation. But they had been told in no uncertain terms not to leave town by the chief inspector of the case, Mitch's old 'friend', Inspector Umberto Dada. Despite having been polished by his fifteen years in the capital into the perfect example of the well-dressed, cynical, and sophisticated big-city detective, Inspector Dada, while not himself of Mayan descent, was originally from the Yucatan state of Quintana Roo, where he had come to know and respect the Mayan people, so he was basically sympathetic to Elena and her cause. But he also knew that his handling of the case would be under the microscope from both the media and his superiors, and he wasn't about to blow fifteen years of careful climbing up the career ladder now, so he was determined to be as thorough and as firm as he needed to be. And while he had no problem accepting Elena's role in the incident and her account of it, he was suspicious of the motives and character of all the gringos involved, Mitch, Teo, and Louis as well as Rick, Billy, and the pilot. But although Mitch could understand the Inspector's attitude and he appreciated the Inspector's gentle treatment of Elena, he still didn't particularly like being under arrest of any kind or Inspector

Dada having his passport, and he thought it was ridiculous anyway since all of the surviving members of the ill-fated expedition were physically and emotionally exhausted and weren't going anywhere for a while. Elena was sustained through the terrible first days of publicity and questions and through her father's funeral by several members of her large, aristocratic family. They seemed very close-knit and caring to Mitch and the way they stood up for Dr Camacho's reputation during the investigation belied the feelings the Professor had that they considered him a black sheep for marrying Elena's mother.

"Oh,well," thought Mitch, "He believed it and he died for it." The press, of course, had a field day with the entire affair. They loved it. The story had everything for them; the jungle, night flights by mysterious airplanes, corrupt gringos, the loyal Professor with the beautiful daughter fighting to save some of their national heritage, violence, and even death. And it played well. The story of the struggling little expedition caught the people's imagination and their case became a "cause célèbre" in the country. Public opinion came down firmly on the side of the Professor and Elena and against the petty bureaucrats who were now seen as obstructing work important to the national consciousness. Consequently several of these bureaucrats and politicians jumped on the bandwagon and vied with one another for the right to praise Dr Comacho at his funeral and in the media. Mitch reflected that the Professor's plan got way out of hand and didn't happen like he wanted, but that he did achieve his goal. Several of these so-called "political leaders" called for new funding on a national level for archeological expeditions and voted new grants to expand the university museum, perhaps with a new wing named for Dr Comacho. Even the money that as the press said "was recovered from that terrible night in the jungle" was donated to the museum and it turned out to be a substantial amount indeed. Elena was the woman of the hour, and Mitch really admired her for the way she handled it. In much the same way that she fought off her lethargy on the coral airstrip when Mitch was in the jungle and she was alone with the guys looking to her, she showed the resiliency and determination that she had gotten from her father and her half-Indian mother. After Dr Comacho's funeral she immersed herself in the project, speaking publicly at every chance and working intently to catalog all the objects and artifacts that had been brought to the museum from Miguel's basement, trying to figure out what was given up and even what was real and what was fake. After a few weeks Mitch and the guys moved back to the Hotel Astoria, with Elena staying at the University to be closer to her work.

Most of this observation of Elena by Mitch was done from afar. During these weeks they barely had a chance to talk to one another, at first because of the police investigation, and then because Elena spent almost all her time working on her father's exhibit at the museum. When they finally did get together for dinner after the guys had moved to the Astoria, it had to be arranged by Teo, who was working closely with Elena daily on the artifacts. On the evening of their dinner, the guys, tired of hanging out at the Astoria every night, had come early to the fashionable downtown restaurant to have a couple of drinks and talk about their situation until Elena arrived. They passed up a booth in favor of sitting and standing at the bar, where they had a better view of the cocktail waitresses coming and going and where they could also watch for Elena. As Teo turned around on his barstool to hand Mitch and Louis their first round of beers, he asked,

"Well, what do you think of our Chief Inspector, this guy Dada? Do you think he is going to give us a fair shake?"

"What do I think of him?" retorted Louis, "I think he thinks he's some kind of Mexican Kojak or something. I mean, those fancy clothes, his hard-ass attitude, all that, then he turns around and is so polite and concerned with Elena, while he's still busting our balls!"

"Well, maybe that's just his style," Teo replied, conciliatory as always, "He does seem to be taking his time and doing a thorough investigation."

"Oh, sure," Mitch replied, putting his

bottle of Bohemia on the bar and then continuing with a sarcastic tone, "He's hell on dead guys and gringo backpackers."

"What do you mean by that?" Teo asked curiously. "Okay, look, he's got Archetti and his men on ice downstairs at the police morgue," replied Mitch bitterly, "And he has us stuck here because he has our passports, but meanwhile Rick's bosses, the sons-of- bitches who caused this whole fiasco, are going on living the good god-damn life in Miami."

"Yeah, that's right," put in Louis, "I heard that Archetti's and the gunman's bodies hadn't been claimed and would probably wind up in pauper's graves out at the city cemetery, and the poor jerk that was flying the plane was so badly burned that they haven't even identified him yet, so no one could claim him if they wanted to."

"Yeah," Mitch observed cynically, "The rich get richer and the poor get dead."

"Come on you guys," replied the ever reasonable Teo, "To be fair to the Inspector, there really isn't much to go on. I mean,

Archetti covered his paper trail pretty well, and Dr Comacho was the only one in our group who knew where the money was really coming from."

"I guess you are right, Teo," Mitch said glumly, "If only we had watched him closer, caught on sooner, asked more questions or something, then maybe we could have done something, anything." He finished his thought by spreading his palms out and shaking his head disconsolately.

"Hey, come on now Mitch," Louis said, putting his hand on Mitch's shoulder, "You know as well as I do that thinking about the 'coulda, shoulda, wouldas' of any situation won't get you anything but old."

"You know, you're right, Louis," Mitch replied smiling, "Let's just have another beer and not worry about it." As Mitch stood up to the bar and motioned to the bartender,

Teo asked, "But what about our passports; do you think we will be getting them back soon?"

"I don't know, Teo," Mitch answered,

"Only Inspector Dada can tell us that, so . . ."

"Hey, speak of the devil," Louis interrupted, "Here's Kojak now." Mitch and Teo turned to see Inspector Dada approaching them across the restaurant.

"How the heck did he find us?" asked a surprised Teo. "That's his job," Mitch replied, "Besides it's no secret that we were coming here tonight. Hey, look on the bright side, maybe he is bringing us our passports, right?" But the guys, including Mitch, weren't feeling as nonchalant as Mitch was trying to act, and they fell silent and shifted uneasily on their barstools as the Inspector approached.

"Good evening, gentlemen," said the dapper detective in greeting as he came up the steps from the restaurant to join them at the bar, "I see that you are beginning to enjoy some of the finer pleasures of life here in the big city."

"Well, uh, yeah, uh, no, well, Mitch is here to have dinner with Elena," stammered Teo, embarrassed by his nervousness but unable to control the urge to explain himself that he felt whenever he was around the Inspector, "Louis and I are just having a couple of beers until she comes." As Teo stopped talking he looked up at Inspector Dada from his barstool and then almost furtively looked away. An amused Inspector Dada just looked at him, a thin smile on his lips, letting the moment stretch out, maybe enjoying the guys discomfort a little and his power to cause it, before saying,

"Relax,Teo, I'm not here to harass you guys, just to talk a little bit. Besides," he went on, "The investigation is going well and you are free to go anywhere you want in this city, so I think this is a good place to meet Elena."

"So, if the investigation is almost over, then when do we get our passports back?" cut in Mitch, standing to look down on the face of the shorter man, then turning to put his bottle on the bar. As Mitch turned back to face him again, the Inspector, unruffled, smiled and calmly shifted his overcoat from one forearm to the other, then patted his upper coat pocket and said,

"Soon, possibly," then his smile faded

quickly as he said, "I just have a few more questions to ask Mitch, privately if he doesn't mind."

"Wait a minute, we are all in this together," broke in Louis, "Whatever happened, we all did it, so you can talk to us all together, no?"

"No, this just concerns Mitch," Inspector Dada replied firmly. Before he could continue Mitch said,

"It's ok, Louis, let's just do whatever he wants, and get this thing over with." Mitch was surprised and worried at first by the Inspector's request but as he walked down the bar the burst of anxious adrenalin he felt was changed to a feeling of put upon aggravation and slow burning anger. So when they got to the end of the bar he whipped around quickly to confront the Inspector, and said, "So what's the deal here, Dada, I mean if you had anything to charge us with you would have done it by now, so you must not have much, huh?"

Something flashed in the black eyes of the solid, stocky detective that made Mitch restrain his urge to poke him in his barrel chest as he made his points, but he was still angry enough to continue with, "So why don't you quit bullshitting around and give us our passports back?" The veteran cop had stood his ground during Mitch's tirade and now he stepped even closer until they were chest to chest, met Mitch's angry gaze firmly and said, "Nothing to go on, huh, well how about conspiracy to smuggle unlicensed antiquities out of the country, which is a felony, then manslaughter, because several deaths occurred during the commission of this felony!" He paused while Mitch turned pale and sank slowly onto the nearest barstool. "So, mister gringo adventurer," he went on, "Your little trip through our beautiful country could take a lot longer than you thought."

"Well," Mitch said nervously, trying to gather his thoughts and hoping he didn't look as scared as he felt, "What do you want from me, I've told you everything I know." The Inspector looked directly into Mitch's, waited a moment and then demanded,

"So why didn't you shoot Mr Archetti when you had the drop on him, heh? You supposedly hated the son-of-a-bitch, didn't you?"

"What do you mean, supposedly?" Mitch said, jumping up again, a little confused, his anger returning, "You mean . . ., you think I was in on it with that rotten bastard! Why? What?"

Inspector Dada just stood by calmly as Mitch started pacing back and forth, then he said, "Well, you are both from South Florida, you're both gringos with no strings attached, and there was big money involved, so . . ."

"And you're saying that I didn't kill him because he was my friend or partner or something, is that it?" Mitch demanded angrily. "Well," he went on, excited now, "I know all about you guys down here and your concept of macho manhood and all that crap, and maybe you can't understand not shooting someone you hate so much, but to me he just wasn't worth it, no way." Mitch paused and tried to get a grip on himself, turning tightly from side to side and clenching and unclenching his fists, then continued to explain as the Inspector just sat and eyed him calmly, "I mean, he had already fucked around with my mind enough, and I didn't want his blood on my hands for the rest of my goddamn life!" Mitch stopped and stood right in front of Inspector Dada, meeting his impassive if slightly skeptical stare directly and saying, "Now that may sound like corny old bullshit to you but that's the way I feel and if you think that that makes me any less of a man, then to hell with you!" As Mitch turned angrily back to the bar and grabbed his beer, the Inspector raised his hand to stop Teo and Louis, who had jumped up at Mitch's outburst and headed down the bar, and said to Mitch,

"Calm down, Mitch, I believe you, I really do." He paused when Mitch turned and gave him an angry, questioning look, then he continued, "I'm sorry to put you through it, but I just wanted to see and be sure for myself. "And," he smiled at Mitch, "I'm even willing to forget about the 'souvenir' incident that caused our first meeting." Mitch settled down onto a barstool, the torrent of anger that had flowed through him leaving him feeling tired and aggravated, and said,   "All right, you believe us, so what happens now?"

He could barely believe that Dada even remembered his little deal with the souvenirs, it seemed so minor and so long ago.

"Well," the Inspector said, motioning for Teo and Louis to join them, "No one is being charged with anything, and I have your passports right here." Here he tapped his top pocket once again, smiled wryly and said, "The higher ups want the case closed, you know, all the loose ends tied up and swept under the rug. So they've ruled that the pilot and Mr Archetti's deaths were from the plane crashing and burning, and that Herman shooting the gunman was a justifiable homicide, so that's it, case closed."

"And what about the rich fuckers in Miami, Rick's bosses?" Mitch reminded him bitterly, "Is anybody going after them?" Inspector Dada just smiled the same knowing, cynical smile, shrugged his shoulders and repeated,

"The higher ups want the case closed, that's all. So here, take your passports and be happy." As the guys all reached anxiously for their passports from where the Inspector had dropped them on the bar, Inspector Dada stepped back and said, "Okay, now you are free to come and go as you please, but do me a favor and try to stay out of trouble, at least until you are out of my jurisdiction, right?" The guys all jumped up at once to assure him of that, and to shake his hand and thank him. Even Mitch, feeling a whole lot better with his passport in his hand, and not really begrudging the Inspector the right to do his job the way he saw it, shook his hand and thanked him sincerely. Just as he let go of Mitch's hand and turned to leave, he paused and asked Mitch, "Well, amigo, what about the second shot, would you have done it?" Mitch stood quietly for a moment, remembering the rage, the hate, and even the fear that he had felt while bursting into that clearing with his gun ready, then he just smiled and shrugged as he said,

"I guess we'll never know, Inspector."

"No, I guess not," replied the Inspector, smiling back. He then shook each of their hands and handed his coat to Teo to hold up for him to put it on, smoothed down the lapels to make sure everything was in place, and strolled casually away, pausing for a short wave at the door and then disappearing. The guys sat in silence for a few seconds after the Inspector's exit, then they all broke out laughing and talking at the same time, slapping each other on the back and checking out their passports happily. They were so excited in fact that they didn't see Elena come in and approach them, but finally Teo spotted her coming up the steps and he said, holding up his papers,

"Look, Elena, we've got our passports back, it's all over at last!"

"I know," she smiled in reply, a lot calmer than any of them, "I ran into Inspector Dada outside. It's great, isn't it?" After they had all settled down some, Mitch and Elena greeted each other like a couple of old friends who hadn't seen each other for a long time, asking how are you doing, how are you feeling, just small talk. After Teo and Louis left they got a table and ordered a bottle of wine. They were relaxed together and Elena smiled a lot, and Mitch thought she never looked more beautiful, especially when she spoke animatedly about the exhibit, but it was clear to both of them that they had left something back there in the jungle, that something in their relationship wasn't the same. Maybe her father's death had changed Elena completely as a person, or maybe Mitch had been getting restless even before the climatic events leading up to the Professor's murder. Perhaps the roller-coaster nature of their affair, the heating and cooling sequence of their passion, plus the whipsawing of their emotions by the stress and demands of their recent situations burned them out, left them just too tired inside to pay the price of maintaining their relationship. Whatever the reason the change was clear to both of them, and neither one seemed to fight it very hard. When Mitch told Elena, as they were finishing their last glass of wine before dessert, of his plans to continue his journey south, she did get emotional, the blinking sting that is the beginning of tears in her eyes as she asked,

"Why don't you stay and help me, help me finish my father's project?" She paused to gulp back her tears, then pleaded, "Mitch, my father gave his life for this cause, and I can't let him down now, let his sacrifice be for nothing, don't you see? When we've been through so much together, we've come this far together . . ." As her voice trailed off Mitch felt a pain in his heart, but he had thought it out during many sleepless nights the last few weeks and he told her,   "Well, there's two things, Elena, first, it's not your father's project now, it's yours. And second, you don't need my help. You are doing pretty darn good all by yourself, and besides, there's Teo and a whole museum staff to help you. Don't you see, you have made a name for yourself, and you have your project, your direction. I care a lot about you Elena, and we have meant something to each other, but you've got your own life now and it means something to you. I could stay and help, but it's your dream, not mine. I don't know what I'll find, but I didn't know what I was looking for when I left, either." He paused and took her hands in his across the table, "I know I won't find a better lady anywhere, but I have got to go . . ." He looked into her eyes and said, "You understand, don't you? Please understand."

The sting in Elena's eyes had turned to real tears now as she asked in a small voice,

"And what if you find this 'Holy Grail', what then? Will you ever be by this way again?" Her deep black eyes were filled with sadness and a kind of knowing resignation as Mitch tried to smile nonchalantly and said,

"All things are possible in this world, my lady." He stood up still holding one of her hands and said, "Come on, let's dance." She held his hand and looked up at him for a long moment and then smiled as she stood and went into his arms.

They held each other the rest of the night in a mood of bittersweet pleasure, neither wanting the night to end but both knowing it must. In the inevitable morning they stood together in the lobby of the Astoria, holding each other past the moment when it would have been easy to let go. Finally Elena stepped back a small step and Mitch let go of her shoulders.

"You had better get going or you will miss your bus," she said, shaking her hair and smoothing her skirt. Mitch started to say something like 'thanks for understanding' but Elena cut him off by raising one finger to his lips. "Vaya con Dios, amigo," she whispered, stared at him for a long moment and then turned and walked away across the lobby. Mitch waited a minute to watch those beautiful legs walk away from him.

"I'm probably being a fool again," he thought as he hitched up his backpack from against the wall, "I don't know where I'm going or what I'm going to do when I get there, but I'm going." As he came out the front door he saw Teo and Louis sitting on the steps, one backpack between them. They jumped up as Mitch approached and Louis asked with a smile,

"Going South, Senor? Me, too."

Mitch nodded, "Sure, come on, partner." He turned to Teo, "What about you, my friend, you coming with us?" Teo grinned and shook his hand as he extended his hand to shake with Mitch.

"No, I'm going to stay here and work on the dig and at the museum, maybe do my Master's thesis on it. Being here is going to be good for my career, and besides, there is no way that I can go back to that chilly old library on campus, at least not for a while." Mitch returned his handshake firmly and replied,

"Sounds good to me, I'm sure you will do a great job with it." He had almost released Teo's hand but instead pulled him in for a big hug, just saying "friends" and then turning to Louis. "You all set?" he asked and when Louis nodded in the affirmative he turned back to Teo and quoted with a smile, "Happy trails to you, amigo, until we meet again!" Teo smiled and said, "I'm sure we will sometime, my friend, meanwhile, vaya con dios and be careful." With that Mitch turned, hitched up his backpack into a more comfortable position and set out once again down the Gringo Trail.

Manufactured by Amazon.ca
Acheson, AB